"What is it?"

"I'm not sure," Miles said. "Don't move, though. And don't touch anything for a minute."

Scarlett walked over to him. "Oh my God. What happened? Is that blood from you?" She grabbed his arm, looking for a cut.

"That's not from me. You and Kelcie hadn't been here yet, right?"

"No. Jackson just checked us into the cabin. I didn't even know where it was."

That didn't mean that Kelcie and Jackson weren't there.

"Was Kelcie bleeding after the accident on the mountain? Could this be from her?"

"She wasn't actively bleeding. Not enough to have left a trail like this, if that's what you're getting at." She started to follow the trail, disappearing around the side of the cabin. "Come here. Look."

He followed. Around the corner, he found bits of glittering glass where it appeared someone had punched in one of the glass panels of the door to let themselves in.

"We need to call the police. I'm sure they're going to be thrilled to speak to me again today."

STALKED IN THE MOUNTAINS

DANICA WINTERS

To my readers,

Thank you for your ongoing support and love.
You are the reasons I write.

Acknowledgments:

A huge shout-out to my team at Harlequin—
without them these books would not be possible. Their hard work and dedication are truly second to none. Thank you for all that you do.

Also, thank you to my team of reviewers. I appreciate each and every review posted for my books. They make a huge difference. Keep them coming.

Recycling programs for this product may not exist in your area.

ISBN-13: 978-1-335-69045-6

Stalked in the Mountains

Harlequin Enterprises ULC
22 Adelaide St. West, 41st Floor
Toronto, Ontario M5H 4E3, Canada
www.Harlequin.com

HarperCollins Publishers
Macken House, 39/40 Mayor Street Upper,
Dublin 1, D01 C9W8, Ireland
www.HarperCollins.com

Printed in Lithuania

Danica Winters is a multiple-award-winning, bestselling author who writes books that grip readers with their ability to drive emotion through suspense and occasionally a touch of magic. When she's not working, she can be found in the wilds of Montana, testing her patience while she tries to hone her skills at various crafts—quilting, pottery and painting are not her areas of expertise. She believes the cup is neither half-full nor half-empty, but it better be filled with wine. Visit her website at danicawinters.net.

Books by Danica Winters

Harlequin Intrigue

West Glacier Ranch Suspense

Rodeo Crime Ring
Mystery on the Range
Stalked in the Mountains

Big Sky Search and Rescue

Helicopter Rescue
Swiftwater Enemies
Mountain Abduction
Winter Warning

STEALTH: Shadow Team

A Loaded Question
Rescue Mission: Secret Child
A Judge's Secrets
K-9 Recovery
Lone Wolf Bounty Hunter
Montana Wilderness Pursuit

Stealth

Hidden Truth
In His Sights
Her Assassin For Hire
Protective Operation

Visit the Author Profile page at Harlequin.com.

CAST OF CHARACTERS

Scarlett Leafletter—A starlet with secrets as big as the Montana sky. Just when she thought she had run away for good, she finds herself back in the wilderness of her childhood home and in the sights of a man she once thought she could trust.

Miles Miller—This handsome cowboy is the main guide for the West Glacier Ranch. Tasked with keeping guests happy is sometimes a job that is easier said than done—especially when keeping a Hollywood glamour girl and her sidekick out of the hands of a potential killer.

Thomas Sullivan—As a returning guest of Miles's, this easy to love five-year-old is one of the toughest hombres around, and this is proven when he is forced to face a series of events that test not only his courage, but also his fortitude and adaptability.

Jackson Miller—New to the ranch and eager to prove himself to his brother Miles, Jackson must work with Kelcie in order to keep Scarlett out of harm's way. Little does he know, but danger is lurking in the shadows and waiting just for them.

Kelcie Sherry—Scarlett's best friend and assistant is there for everything in her life, but when she disappears, they all fear the worst and they must work fast to find out what has happened to the missing woman.

Chloe Purvis—As Miles's ex-girlfriend and near miss, he has any number of reasons to despise her, but hate and love can sometimes make for strange results.

Butch Hafner—Scarlett's former agent turned stalker. As ugly as he is dangerous, the rat has a way of sticking to the darkness and rarely being seen—which constantly keeps Scarlett wondering if the battles she faces are merely in her head, or if this war is really because he is the one pulling the strings.

Chapter One

Scarlett Leafletter never wanted a child. She didn't want the incessant wailings of a newborn, the sleepless nights, a toddler clawing on her legs, or the disgusting and messy battle of potty training.

She didn't begrudge any woman who wanted the life—no, far from it. In fact, those women deserved statues in their honor instead of simply one day a year when they were forced to choke down runny eggs with shells and half-cooked pancakes.

There had never even been a fleeting moment as a teenager when she'd envisioned herself setting the table for her husband and children after cooking the traditional dinner and conforming to the gender roles that usually came with rural Montana living. Especially as one got deeper into farming and ranching country.

Scarlett had grown up smack-dab in the center of nowhere and grab-your-husband's-slippers, and she had gotten out of there as soon as she'd tossed her graduation cap into the air—so fast, she wasn't sure she'd even seen the thing hit the ground.

Her parents hadn't understood her rush, but they also hadn't seen the girls in her high school. When she'd graduated, there were thirty girls in her class. Five had already gotten pregnant and had their first kid—all with members of the football team. Ten others had decided to get married to their high school boyfriends, most of whom had dropped out a year or two before them and had gone to work on one of the many wheat ranches on the other side of the continental divide. Only three of the girls she'd graduated with, including herself, had plans to go to college.

One of the three had already screwed up and just found out she'd accidentally gotten pregnant—and that, right there, had been why Scarlett had never been one to drink to excess. The only other girl who had made it out of West Glacier High School and their tiny town had ended up married to a super sweet woman five years ago after she had become an orthopedic nurse in Missoula. She and Scarlett were still friends, but only in passing and on social media.

So the last thing she'd expected was to find herself facing a near-miss pregnancy, a mess of a personal life and thinking about running home with her hat figuratively in hand.

There was no way she could tell them she was coming—if she had they would have turned her and her assistant away at the airport. Heck, they would probably meet her with a mob complete with pitchforks and shotguns. Her sister, Jamie, and her brother Cameron were the only ones at the ranch now, and the last time she had seen Cameron they had been throwing hands.

Ever since their father had been killed and major drama had unfolded at the West Glacier Cattle Ranch, she had been following the news out of Kalispell that had been twisting tales about their infamous ranch. It had seemed in the last two years since Cameron, and now Jamie, had taken the reins that things had started to take a turn for the better financially.

The latest headline announced they were opening the ranch up for guests and for a new foundation called JMac, an equine therapy program geared toward children. Both were booking out for this summer. It was that headline, and some fortuitous timing in her personal life, that had beckoned her home like she was some kind of goddamned lost lamb.

She just wasn't sure if she was ready to go there—if she went home, she had a feeling she was coming home for slaughter.

Her phone rang. She hit Ignore when she saw the screen, and then she blocked the caller. A minute later it happened again, but this time the number had changed. This repeated another ten times before she finally just turned off the device and tossed the damned thing into her purse. It made a loud *ting*—it must have hit the black bottle of YSL perfume she always kept inside next to her wallet.

Her cell phone company was going to get tired of seeing her face. This would be the fifth time she would have to go into the store to change her phone number.

"If you're not careful, you're going to bust that bottle one of these days—not to mention it may cost you a new phone… again." Her best friend and personal assistant, Kelcie Sherry, came sauntering out of the back bedroom of the hotel suite carrying a makeup bag and a handful of brushes. "You already used up your free insurance phone claims for the year, and mine. No more breaking them. It's going to start getting expensive."

She waved off her friend. This thing with her agent—well, her *ex-agent*—had already gotten expensive and obnoxious. She had been hoping he would get the hint that she really wasn't interested in taking things anywhere near the bedroom with his Harvey Weinstein ass, but clearly, he wasn't getting the picture.

Ever since she had rebuffed his advances at the wrap party for this season of *Rogue Crafter*, things between them had gotten worse. What had been a call a day and maybe ten to twenty texts, which she had thought was already quite a bit for an agent, suddenly turned to twenty calls and hundreds of inane texts about nothing.

The night of the party six months ago, there had been an open bar and exposed secrets. He'd thought their conversation had been an invitation into her heart and pants when in reality it had been nothing more than a miscalculation of who she thought she could trust.

She would like to say she had learned her lesson, and she had moved on, but even though she had let him go as her film agent and put her career on hold to do so, his behavior hadn't stopped.

Right now, he was probably sending her a flurry of messages on one of the social media platforms because her voicemail was full. The thought of him scrolling through all her pictures, many of which he had taken as part of her "portfolio," made her stomach roil and a bit of acid move up into her throat. She could taste the bile.

What a fool she had been to let a predatory man like him into her life.

When she'd been signed by him and the Cucco Film Agency—he was the sole owner—she'd thought she'd finally broken into the big leagues in the world of acting. He had gotten her one of her first roles in television, a commercial for yogurt. She still had a copy of it somewhere downloaded on her laptop. If she couldn't find it, she was sure she could get it on YouTube.

It was funny how much time had not really passed, but with film years being like dog years, it seemed like a lifetime. Since then, her stock in the industry had exploded—and he had leveraged his role in her life to keep her not only as a client but as a supplicant. It had been a strange, codependent and well-groomed relationship. One that, until she'd been pulled out of and seen others' *normal* relationships with their agents, she hadn't understood for the toxicity that it had been.

Now she was in damage control.

"Kelcie, would you hand me my computer?" she asked, motioning toward the bag on the floor by the glass door that led out onto the balcony.

The hotel the studio had been putting them up at was beautiful in Santa Barbara, and from where she sat, she had a view of the ocean and a smattering of palm trees. They really had pulled out all the stops this time. Maybe they knew they had underpaid her by thirty thousand dollars. It was fine—when she got a new agent, she would make sure the next one was a pit bull when it came to negotiations.

She pulled up the website for her family's ranch. It drew up the sting of familiar memories as she saw the old barn, where she had spent more than a few nights hiding from her parents, and the beaverslides from her grandparents' farming days. If nothing else, she could dream about the foothills of the steep mountains and the smell of the pine pollen in the air. Though she wasn't a cowgirl by any stretch, there were things about that world she had always loved. Country living did have its charms.

On the front page of the website there was a link to adventure rides and something about the new equine therapy program. She clicked on the adventure rides link, and it led her straight to the picture of a man holding the reins of a beautiful gray mare. As stunning as the horse was, the man was a thousand times better. According to the little write-up beneath, the man was one of the guides for their trail rides and his name was Miles Miller. Even his name was cute.

The marketers behind the ranch had made a mistake not putting him on the landing page, because his face was one that could have launched a thousand ships—or at least a thousand women on planes, trains and automobiles into the back-country.

Though she tried to avoid her email, it popped up. She was flooded with emails from Butch. So far, there were thirty-seven. The first were innocuous enough. Why didn't you answer? to Are you okay? But as she got to the most recent, they rapidly devolved into threats, and the last read, You stupid witch. You'd be nothing without me. I'm glad you lost your baby.

Another email popped up from him just as she exited out and opened a new browser. He could take his emails, his phone calls, voicemails and texts and stick them all where the sun didn't shine.

She needed to get out of California and as far away from him as possible.

She pulled up her Alaska Airlines account. Using some of her hundreds of thousands of miles, she booked them on the first flight to Montana.

Butch's Facebook profile pic popped up on the corner of her screen just as she was finishing up their reservations. There were the little dots indicating he was typing. It didn't take long for him to send his message: I'm going to kill you.

She had never thought she would run away from danger, but there was no safer place in her mind than the backcountry of Montana—and, if push came to shove, there was no better place to hide an enemy's body.

Chapter Two

Healing a broken heart was like attempting to train a shark while there was blood in the water. A person could try but they were probably going to only get really hurt—and wound others in the process.

Miles Miller wouldn't have considered himself the sensitive kind. In fact, he was about as far from emotional as a cow's tail was from its nose. Sure, once in a while he'd brush up against a feeling, but it left him wishing he'd never touched the damned thing as it had a way of leaving a whole lot of crap behind.

After this last relationship with Chloe Purvis, he wouldn't be dating for a long, long time. He looked down at the ring on the top of his dresser as he grabbed out a pair of fresh Wrangler jeans. She had made such a big, damned deal about wanting to get engaged and getting a ring and then he'd never even gotten a chance to ask. She had decided to kick him to the curb and start dating his former boss at the Joy Luck Ranch on the other side of Flathead Valley. In retaliation, he had taken the head guide position at their largest competitor, the West Glacier Ranch.

He smiled at the thought of how much it probably ticked off his old boss, Drake Rex.

Just today, he had what was left of the Sullivan family coming out. They normally visited the Joy Luck every summer, but after Catherine Sullivan had passed away last fall, her husband, Aiden, had jumped ship to follow Miles. Aiden wanted to get his son, Thomas, involved with the youth equine therapy program to help him through the grief of losing his mother.

Miles loved his new job and the possibilities of more that came with it. Cameron had been great, his wife, Deputy Emily Trapper, was always a kick, and Jamie had given him pretty much free rein when it came to helping her to run the equine therapy program. She was away on a retreat for the day and wouldn't be back until at least tomorrow or perhaps two more days, depending on how things went.

He pulled on his jeans and cinched his belt tight. His silver belt buckle had been a hand-me-down from his grandfather's rodeoing days, and it had a gold bull on its face with a nearly illegible engraving that read Cheyenne Frontier Days 1973. His grandfather Dickie Cox hadn't been the overall champion that year, but he'd taken home the championship buckle in bull riding and had worn the thing every day until he'd passed. It had been given to Miles with the caveat that he wear it as much as possible to keep his grandfather's memory alive.

He'd embraced the buckle, the task and the honor with both hands and an open heart. He'd worshiped the ground his grandfather's boots had touched. When he'd been young, everywhere they'd gone, his grandfather had gotten free coffee and lunch, and people had wanted to talk about "the old days." Jamie had loved it, thanks to her rodeoing past, and he held no doubts it was part of the reason he and his brother Jackson had gotten jobs at the ranch.

Even now, when Miles was out with the guests, he'd always end up telling them all about his grandfather and his days on the rodeo circuit. In some ways, it felt as though it was stolen valor. He'd never made it in the world of bull riding—his mother hadn't wanted him to go down that dangerous path.

Between relationships and bull riding, she'd been wrong about which would bring the most danger.

He took one last look at the diamond ring. The one saving grace about the damned thing was that it had never really been hers. If only he was a better bull rider, he would have sold it for an entrance fee in the Cheyenne Rodeo so he could have a run at winning his own buckle. At least that way, one way or another, he could have honored his grandfather's memory.

He slipped on his cowboy hat as he walked out of the bunkhouse. Today he was the last one out. There were only two other hands that lived in the bunkhouse, but if he had his way, soon his brother Brent, Andrew, Xander and Gus would all be working the place along with him.

It was a bit of a haul up to the barn in the pickup. When he arrived, there were two women lolling about by the green steel gates leading into the main pasture. The blonde lady was breaking handfuls off the tall, green grass outside the fence and feeding it to MacGyver, Jamie's horse. She was scratching the blaze marking on the gelding's forehead as the horse nibbled at the grass in her hand and she whispered sweet nothings into the big man's ear.

He seemed to be eating up the attention.

The woman's friend was tapping on her phone. She looked out of place in Montana, with her big brown purse with some guy's name written on it, gold hoop earrings and a fur-edged jacket that was so big, if she actually did need it to keep warm it wouldn't hold any warmth in—it fit her like a giant collapsible canvas wall tent.

But the woman did have a beautiful white felt hat. He could tell it had never touched the ground, but it did wonders for her brunette hair and olive-hued skin. She was out of his league, as she could have been a model for any one of the fashion websites his ex used to scroll through, but undeniably stunning.

He got out of the pickup and strolled over toward them. "Good morning, ladies," he said, touching the brim of his cowboy hat and giving them a tip of the head in greeting. "How y'all doing today?"

The one feeding MacGyver jerked like she hadn't heard his truck pull up or him making his way over to them. The other just looked annoyed. He glanced down at his watch. None of the guests on today's ride were supposed to have been there for another hour, so he wasn't exactly sure why they would be annoyed with *him*.

"*We're* cold." The one in the jacket pranced over to him in her too-tall heels, carefully picking through the dirt and muck in front of the barn.

For spring, it was unseasonably warm, but when it came to the ranch's guests, he'd learned not to point out the obvious—it didn't help him earn his tips. He was here only to make them happy and to serve them and let them have the experience of their lives, nothing less.

"If you're cold, I can take you back to your cabins to warm up—if you are staying on the ranch. I won't be ready for us to head out on the trail for another hour or so."

"We're not booked into a cabin yet. Let's see how the ride goes first." The sour but beautiful woman scowled. "We were told the horses would be ready at eight o'clock. It's eight now. Do things always run late on this ranch?"

And they were off to the races.

This was clearly not going to be one of his favorite outings.

He did a quick recalculation of the map route he'd intended on taking them on with the horses—if he stopped before last corner, they could cut three miles and at least an hour off their time together. *Perfect.*

In fact, if he could get Jackson or one of the Trappers to take this group…

He glanced toward the main ranch house, but there was no one outside and the trucks that were normally parked around it were already gone for the day. Jackson wouldn't be back to the barn from checking on the cattle up in the high pastures for at least a couple more hours.

Today would be all on him.

He checked his sigh before facing the firing squad that was Ms. Model. "We pride ourselves on working on time, efficiently and as safely as possible here at the West Glacier Ranch. I'm sorry to tell you, but it's actually only seven o'clock I'm afraid you have the wrong time."

The model waved him off, her fingernails catching the light and showing off the white tips. Everything about this woman had been coifed and buffed. She wouldn't last a minute on this ranch if she was left to her own devices. "That's impossible. Everything is digital and updates automatically."

He shrugged. "Well, ma'am, that may be true in most places around the world, but we often run into technological snafus here in the high country—sorry to tell ya." He tried to sound apologetic for something he actually kind of loved. He appreciated the fact that tech was still something that had to be sought out instead of instantly accessible every second of the day. "I will have everything ready in an hour."

She looked furious.

He needed to turn things around before he heard about it from Cameron. The last thing they needed was a bad review on their new guest services—and this woman looked like exactly the type who would go out of her way to sink a burgeoning business just because he'd annoyed her.

"By the way, my name is Miles Miller," he said, extending his hand.

She looked at his calloused hands and dirt-stained fingers for a long moment. "Miles." She clipped his name. "That's Kelcie Sherry. She's my personal assistant." She put her hand in his for a brief second and gave it a weak shake. "As for me, I'm Scarlett Leafletter."

The name was so strange, but he simply nodded. "Nice to meet you, Ms. Leafletter."

"You may call me Scarlett." She pushed her loose brunette hair back over the fur collar of her jacket with a twitch of the head like a headstrong mare.

"We are waiting for a father and son to join us for the ride today."

She huffed. "I was hoping to make it a private ride. Is there any way we can make it happen?"

He shook his head. If there was any way he could come up with to unload this woman on anyone else at the ranch, he would have done it. "Unfortunately, all our hands are out working today and assisting other guests. The Sullivan family booked their trip nearly six months in advance. According to my emails, you booked *yesterday*."

Again, he was met with that ridiculous flip of the hand to wave him off.

She would be riding at the back of the group.

"You're welcome to join me in the barn while I get things ready. If I don't get moving, we really won't get out on time," he said, trying to remind himself to be patient.

He saddled up six of his favorite horses. He made sure to pick a headstrong mare for the headstrong woman. It was strange, but often two like-minded beasts tended to work the best together. It was as if somewhere along the line in their push-and-pull they developed mutual respect and from there a good working relationship. If he didn't work it that way, one often had a way of running over the other and neither the horse nor the person had a good experience.

As he was tightening the straps on the last mare's saddle, Scarlett pranced over. "Are we going to have a chef with us for the day?" She looked around the ground expectantly, like Gordon Ramsey was going to pop up from behind one of the horses to join them.

"Yes, that would be *me*." He sent her a wide, sarcastic smile, though he was more than aware he was pressing his luck with this city woman.

She gave him a slow look up and down, sizing him up, and then she glanced back down at his hands where they rested on the saddle. "I guess you really are a jack-of-all-trades."

For the first time since he'd met her this morning, the words coming out of her mouth weren't entirely off-putting. She still looked at him with a bit of hostility. However, based on her tone, he would have almost thought it was something approaching a compliment. She had him confused.

"I'm the man those around me need me to be," he said, sending her a smile he hoped would melt away any ice that still rested between them.

She gave a slight nod. "I can tell. Your bosses must be happy to have you on staff."

There it was—a genuine compliment. What was happening?

Did she need something?

He was still going to make her ride in the back of the string.

"I don't know if I've been around long enough for them to go on and be thinking that." He gave an uncomfortable laugh. He wasn't used to being complimented by good-looking women. "I'm gonna step into the barn here and start gettin' the horses ready."

"Do you mind terribly if I tag along?" She looked over her shoulder, toward the main road.

Something about it struck him as odd, but he brushed it off. City girls were strange creatures, and he had never been one to understand them. They tended to see things that he wasn't used to looking for and vice versa.

"You're welcome to join me. Kelcie, too." He motioned toward the blonde who was petting Mac.

Kelcie turned toward him at the mention of her name. "I'm good. I'll just pet the horse, if that's okay."

He smiled. "That boy's name is MacGyver. He's a retired barrel racing horse and he'll eat up all the attention you want to put on him." He motioned for Scarlett to follow him as he slid open the heavy red doors. They squeaked as the casters moved on the steel rails overhead.

She took off her coat as they walked into the barn.

"Here, let me take that for you." He took it and her purse and hung them on the hook for the bridles just inside the barn door.

There was a clink of glass and keys. He could only guess what the woman was carrying in the bag that was nearly as large as the panniers he used on the pack mules.

There was the sound of a truck pulling up and doors slamming. The mare he was working with lifted her head and gave out a long exhale, then shook her head. Even she could tell it was going to be a long, exhausting day.

The princess beside him walked over to the mare he'd chosen for her, the buckskin quarter horse with mustang lineage, and started to scratch the area right above the mare's tail. The horse lifted her foot slightly and softened with Scarlett's touch.

"So, you know horses?" he asked.

She nodded. "Some. The last series I worked on, we worked out of Belarus. I had four different horses that I rode for the show. By the end of the shoot, I really wanted to bring my favorite girl home, but the owners of the horse wouldn't sell."

"You're a star?" He should have known. With a name like hers and a persona like that, she had pain in the ass written all over her.

She smiled, but the humble look he assumed she was going for didn't quite make it to her eyes. He could see pride in them, but he couldn't begrudge her—he had no doubt she had worked hard for her position in life. Yet, she was wrong if she had thought she was the only one who worked hard in this world.

"I've done three television series—I've even won an Emmy." She sent him a charming smile.

"You looked familiar," he lied. "Thought I knew the name, but I don't get a lot of downtime to watch TV, ya know?"

She seemed mollified by his answer as she scratched the horse. "I'm sure. I don't get a lot of time to come out here and do this kind of thing, either."

For a fleeting moment, Miles found himself surprised, for in this second, he'd found a common thread with the most uncommon of people—and, he could almost say he'd found the mustard seed of friendship.

Chapter Three

The cowboy who she'd thought looked so handsome on the internet was even more striking in person. It was just too bad he seemed to have taken an instant disliking to her. He wasn't the first.

In her world, it seemed like people took one look at her and decided to either love or hate her, and there was no bringing them back from the dark side once they decided. It was too bad. Having him along to flirt with for the horseback trip would have been a fun diversion—and she was pretty good at charming people, if she said so herself.

Sickeningly enough, she had a stalker to prove it.

That wasn't funny. It really wasn't. However, months ago she had resigned herself to a sick sense of humor to deal with the problems she had been facing in her job.

Though she hated to admit it, she had probably brought the agent's unwanted advances upon herself. If she hadn't played into the gender roles maybe she wouldn't have sent her career into a full tailspin complete with this fireball that was the cowboy at the end.

She had just wrapped up filming her last season for the new show on the Syfy network, *Rogue Crafter.* If the show didn't find a solid footing with viewers, her career would be as good as over. She didn't have an agent anymore. Which in her world meant she wouldn't get pitched for possible roles. Which meant she didn't get any other acting jobs.

Her emotions caught in her throat.

She had worked so hard and sacrificed so much to become an actress—she had even given up Montana. One jerk without boundaries and the ability to hear "no" had killed her dreams.

She was angry on so many levels, but firstly at herself for making it so easy for some guy to take her out at the knees. In her head, she was so much stronger than she had proven herself to be.

Her horse moved, exhaled hard and shook the nerves off as the group started forward. Of course the fireball cowboy, Miles, had put her at the back of the line. He mustn't want to be anywhere near her. He probably thought she was going to whine and complain and didn't want to hear any of it. Clearly, he didn't have a clue who she really was.

The saddlebags were making a loud squeaking noise as her mare, Seagrass, moved. It was a leathery sound, but as they moved, the *squeak, squeak, squeak* made her want to drive a nail into her eardrum.

She moved to pull her phone out of her jacket pocket, but then she remembered that she had taken off her adorable Gucci jacket after Miles had said it would spook the horses. Clearly, he didn't understand fashion, and he underestimated horses.

Instead of taking out her phone, she reached forward and gave her girl a nice scratch to the side of her bobbing neck. She did love horses. She always had, though she was nowhere near the rider her barrel racing sister had always been and would be. The thought made Scarlett miss her.

She touched the tip of her nose. If her sister, Jamie, had seen her on the ranch, she was sure that she would have recognized her, but she had been careful in planning. According to the man she had spoken to when booking, her sister was out of town today, so if she was careful, they would never cross paths.

As for the rest of her family, they weren't actively running the guests' section of the ranch. All she had to do was keep out of the way and she could go unnoticed. It wasn't like she was there under her real name. Even if her brother did see her, she wasn't sure how he would react—he would probably kick her out. If he had wanted her back here, he would have reached out when their father had passed away.

The lack of care from her siblings and family stung. Regardless of the fights in their past, she would have thought that one of them would have reached out to let her know about their father's and brother's passing. She deserved to be informed and to have had the choice to come back for the services. That was, assuming they had services—she didn't really know what they had done, given the circumstances of their deaths.

The smell of horses permeated the air as one of the animals in front of her made itself lighter for their ride. Miles probably thought it was hilarious watching her deal with the realities that came with this kind of world. Well, he could laugh at her all he wanted. She wouldn't let him see she was bothered. Kelcie looked back at her over her shoulder, and she crinkled her nose in disgust. Scarlett laughed like it was nothing, and she caught Miles's gaze as she did. Put one on the board for the starlet.

As she relaxed, Seagrass picked up pace and tried to pass the gelding on the right to move to the front of the string. She seemed annoyed with being forced to be in the back of the pack. Scarlett pulled her back. The mare threw her a backward ear and pressed hard against the reins, checking her rider to see who was really in control.

The mare had another think coming if she thought she could take her for a ride. She wasn't the best rider on the ranch, but second only to the guide, she was the greatest in the group, and she wasn't about to let a horse best her.

The family of two in front of them was talking about horses and Glacier National Park and the bear they had seen one time that was *just huge*. So far, the kid hadn't stopped talking. The more she listened the more she was convinced it really wasn't that big and was probably nothing more than a black bear cub, but she didn't interrupt. It was cute listening to the five-year-old boy, Thomas, talk about the bear like it was the coolest thing he had ever seen in his entire life.

If only Scarlett could go back there, to those days and that level of innocence.

Instead, she was in the darkest moment of her life, passing through a cloud of stink while looking for answers and a means for escape.

When she'd left the ranch, she had thought life couldn't get harder, but now she knew that wasn't true. Life had one hell of a way of looking at a person at their lowest and saying, "I can beat that… Hold my beer and watch this."

The only saving grace, at least now, was that she had some financial freedom. When she'd left, she hadn't had two dimes to rub together.

Her mind wandered as she thought about her past and her days spent on the ranch. It was strange, but as they moved up the trail that led toward Glacier National Park, she couldn't remember ever having been on this pathway before. She was sure if they followed it for a full day, it would take them all the way into the park. But Miles had told them they were only going to be skirting the edges as it was just a day trip, and they would have to ride back to the ranch.

From inside the saddlebag where her coat and purse were

stuffed, she could hear her phone ringing, and ringing, and ringing. A part of her felt a deep satisfaction that she couldn't pick up and that something else and *someone* else had stopped her from being at Butch's beck and call.

If he knew she'd left California and his immediate grasp, he would be so angry. And, if he found out she was in Montana…it would make him beyond rabid—he would go straight for her jugular.

In their many travels abroad together, she had talked about her childhood and her parents. He'd been her sounding board, and she'd revealed pains of her past that she couldn't remember sharing with anyone else. Now, if he knew she was here, he would use all those secrets against her and tell her what an idiot she was for coming here—how weak she had become in falling back into the safety net of Montana. In that, he wouldn't have been wrong. She did feel weak running home. Yet, he had left her with no other moves. He'd put her in check.

Her horse flicked its ear toward her like it could sense her unease, and it gave a long huff beneath her thighs. Then it shook, forcing out some of their shared anxiety.

The medley of thoughts about Butch, her family, the cowboy, Kelcie, her job, her love life, her living situations…all of it…could wait. For now, she needed to enjoy the pines around her, the clip-clop of the horses' shoed footfalls on the packed earthen trail, and the view of the cowboy's Wrangler-covered behind in the saddle in front of them.

As though he could sense her looking at him, Miles moved to the side and let the family take the lead. He pointed up the trail, probably telling the father to just keep going. He pulled his horse to a stop and waited for her as she and Kelcie moved up the trail toward him. As soon as she reached him, he started forward at her side. "How's it going? You've been pretty quiet back here."

"Just picking up the slack back here, no problems." She smiled, trying to hide the fact she hated being last at anything.

"Seagrass is normally a nipper. I'm surprised you're not having a bit of a rodeo back here."

She lifted a brow. "If you know my horse has a biting problem, why would you put her in the back?" She knew the answer before she even asked, but she had to see his reaction. She needed to know who this man really was—and what kind of ego she was dealing with.

He sent her a guilty smirk—it was dangerously sexy, and she was torn as to whether she wanted to slap or kiss the smile from his lips. For the time being, she settled on looking down to Seagrass and pretending not to be taken by the handsome cowboy.

He rode ahead and turned in the saddle to address everyone. "Let's stop here and have a little lunch," he said, motioning toward a small meadow.

She had been so wrapped up with the cowboy, staying straight in the saddle and going through all the things in her mind that she hadn't really paid attention to the ride. As the group came to a halt, there was a wooden hitching post grayed with age and weather. The ground around it had been trodden to bare dirt and mud thanks to what must have been a regular stream of horses and riders.

Though she was completely capable, she waited for a moment for Miles to help Aiden and Thomas to dismount and tie up. Then he made his way over to her. He held Seagrass steady, though the horse was like a rock and didn't budge as she swung her leg over and stepped down. She gave the horse a pet as he tied her up.

"How are you doing? Hips and back okay? I know riding

can be hard on the body when you're not used to it," Miles asked, giving her a kind smile.

The smile was one that had probably melted the clothes off many a guest and even more buckle bunnies.

Thomas, the blond five-year-old, came bouncing over in a half run, half skip. "Heya, whatcha doing? Did you know there's a river thingy over there?" He pointed vaguely to the right. "And there looks like there's been all kinds of animals. From my tracking app, I think there's been at least three deer, an elk and a rabbit. Do you wanna see?" He talked so fast that it took a second to make sense of everything he was saying.

The kid was undeniably cute and could have probably been cast as the precocious but darling kid in some Hallmark movie, but she wasn't about to fall for his charms.

He slipped his hand into hers. "Come see the river, Ms. Scarlett." He tugged on her as she looked at Miles.

He chuckled as he waved her on. "Go ahead. I'll set up our picnic. You guys go. Lunch will be ready in a few." He turned toward Kelcie and started to help her down. "Why don't you go ahead with her, as well? I can tell she is chomping at the bit to play with that kid."

She hated that her discomfort must have been visible on her features.

It wasn't that she *disliked* kids, it was just that she had so much life that she wanted to live. As it stood, she'd only been to four of the seven continents. A kid would only slow her down.

"Kelcie?" She called for a lifeline.

"Come on!" Thomas urged.

Her assistant laughed as she pointed toward the scowling kid who was now tugging violently on her arm. "I don't think he wants anyone but you."

She sighed, resigning herself to the fact that for the next

few minutes she would be a child's plaything, and she would just have to suck it up. "All right, Thomas."

His hand was sticky with sweat and something unnamable, and it took all her willpower not to extract her hand and wipe it on her jeans. She could only guess at the number and types of bacteria and germs on his hands.

Don't touch your face, she thought, cringing as she hurried along behind him.

There was a thicket of willows heavy with green leaves. The grass along the edges of the stream bank was knee-high, and mixed throughout were the purple flowers that came with June and the red sprigs of Indian paintbrush. There was a pang of childhood memories, as she recalled picking bunches of them and giving them to her mother.

There was a yellow flower—she didn't remember their exact name—but her mother had loved the soft leaves of the plant. Actually, if she recalled, her mom had called them mule's ears, but she doubted that was their scientific name.

"Thomas," she said, pulling the boy gently to a stop.

"Yeah?" he asked.

"You see that flower there?" she asked, pointing toward the gray-green plant with palmate leaves and the densely packed purple pea-shaped blooms.

"Uh-huh?"

"That's called a lupine. Soon, they get pea pods and then they dry out and they *explode*."

"No way!" He let go of her and dropped down to his knees next to the plant, picking one of the blooms.

She smiled. "It's not ready yet, but I promise it's super cool. If you're really quiet, you can hear all these little things bursting in the late summer. It kinda sounds like popcorn popping, but it's the plant sending out its seeds for the next year."

"That's cool."

"Yeah. They're my favorite flower. You know…anything that *explodes*." She held out her hand and helped him to stand up.

He slipped his sticky hand back into hers. "It's my favorite, too."

She felt her Grinch heart grow three sizes, not that she would have admitted it to another living soul.

He looked up at her as he handed her the flower. "This is for you, Ms. Scarlett. I like you."

She took the stem and gently spun the spiked flower in her fingers. It was sad, but she couldn't remember the last time anyone but Butch had given her a gift. "Thank you, sweetheart. I like you, too." She awkwardly patted him on the head, the flower bopping his ear and making him squirm.

As they giggled, they weaved through the thicket of the willows toward the babbling sound of the moving water until they broke through and found what turned out to be nothing close to a river; instead it was a meandering high-mountain stream. The bottom was covered with smooth stones in a rainbow of colors, and as the sun shone through the clear, clean water, it looked like something from an art studio instead of real life.

"Wow," she said, not meaning to speak.

"Isn't it cool, Ms. Scarlett?" Thomas bounced excitedly from foot to foot as he looked up at her and then back down at the thicket and creek around them.

"Thomas, it's perfect. You are quite the explorer, buddy."

His smile faded. "That's what my mom used to say."

And just like that, she was reminded of the conversation she had overhead between the boy's father, Aiden, and Miles. Apparently, they had come here as part of Jamie's equine therapy program to help the boy recover from the loss of his mother.

She was so not equipped to help this boy deal with his loss—she could barely deal with the drama in her own life. If she was, she wouldn't have found herself standing in Montana.

She watched him play at the edge of the stream for a few minutes. She couldn't quite see what he was doing, but he seemed content and happy in his play, and given the reason he was here she felt righteous in allowing him the freedom to continue.

After a bit, there was a cattle call whistle from the distance. It made a shiver of unexpected excitement run down her spine. There was something about that sound that she had always loved. Perhaps it was just so commanding, but it was also sexy.

She couldn't help but smile, and it struck her that perhaps she was here for equine therapy of her own. "Hey, Thomas, why don't we go ahead and head back for lunch?" she asked.

He looked at the water as he shoved something into his pocket.

She cleared her throat. "I'll race you," she said, trying to convince him it was a good idea.

"Okay!" he said, taking off on the trail that they had followed in through the brush.

She made sure to watch him as they broke through the thicket and back into the meadow. He beat her by a landslide.

As she jogged toward the red-checkered blanket that was spread out beneath a large pine, Miles stood there and smiled. No matter how good-looking this white-hatted cowboy was, she couldn't fall for that man. In some ways, falling for him would be even more dangerous than the man who had made her go on the run.

Chapter Four

The way Scarlett's hair picked up the sunshine made it shine like brown satin. Though he would have expected her to be smiling, the expression on her face made it look like she had just left the dentist's office.

She must have really hated running, but damn did she look good while doing it.

He shouldn't have been checking out a guest, but there wasn't really any harm in window shopping. If anything, it would help him to forget all the reasons he could think of to never jump into a relationship again. From the way her body bounced as she ran, he could definitely think of all the reasons he could jump into bed. Sure, that wasn't the best way to start a relationship, but in the world of love, he'd recently learned there were no clear-cut rules.

She came to a skidding stop with Thomas. He wrapped himself around his father's legs and giggled as Scarlett turned away from him and bent over like she was catching her breath. Watching her bend was too much. He had to look away, in an effort not to look like some kind of pervert.

He made his way over to the horses.

There, across from where he'd tied them up, was a trail camera. He watched the shutter flicker open and closed as it took stills. Up here, the camera could have belonged to any number of people, including the Forest Service, who sometimes ran counts on the number of riders who moved through an area.

Trail cameras weren't that uncommon in the area. Hunters used them to watch game animals, hikers used them to check their trails, and even he had used them in the past to track animals so he could make sure to take guests to areas they would be sure to see specific animals on their "must-see" lists. They were a handy tool. However, something about this camera made him feel uncomfortable. He couldn't explain exactly why—perhaps it was merely the fact he had actually noticed the device. Often, the person who'd placed them made sure to do it in such a way that a person or animal never noticed, as it kept the camera from being stolen or vandalized.

He tried to ignore the way the hair on the back of his neck stood up as he thought about the invasion of privacy. It wasn't like the owner of the camera was taking pictures inside his bedroom. He was in public—they had every right to take any picture they wanted.

He ran his hand down his mare, taking a moment to scratch her favorite spot right above the base of her tail. She let out a long exhale and shook her head as she relaxed.

Miles's phone pinged as he put away the cooler of sandwiches into the saddlebag on his mare. She looked back at him with annoyance at the sound. "I know, lady, I don't want to hear that nonsense out here, either." He laughed, pulling the phone from the pocket of his plaid shirt. "And make sure to give the camera your good side," he said, giving her a little slap on the hind quarter.

The phone pinged with a second message. At the point in the day, the phone call could have been just about anyone, but he hoped it wasn't one of the Trappers. They were nice to work for and pretty good bosses, but if he was on the trail and they were texting it only meant one thing—he was in trouble.

Unlocking the screen his stomach sank. It was worse—it was the ex, Chloe.

He wasn't sure he really wanted to ruin his day by reading her messages, but sometimes the best thing to do with a splinter was to pull it out. If not, it had a way of festering.

He squeezed his eyes shut and then sucked in a breath as he summoned the strength to face the unknown as he tapped open the phone.

You're a thief now? The Sullivans are clients of the Joy Luck. How dare you steal our business!

Of course, Chloe would think the worst of him. She would never take responsibility for her role in their breakup or the fact that she had cheated on him. Now she had the audacity to act like she had any skin in the game when it came to the business of the ranches.

He scrolled to the next message.

How many other clients have u stolen? We're watching. This better be it.

He glanced up at the trail camera, wondering if the device was one of theirs. There was a deep urge to flip the thing the bird, but he reminded himself that Thomas may have been watching. Besides, he wasn't afraid of her empty threats. Chloe didn't have any teeth. If the ranch owner had texted, Drake, he would have been slightly more concerned—but even then, he had never known the guy for anything other than being full of hot air.

It wasn't Miles's fault the clientele had followed him to his new home. At least at the West Glacier, he was treated right.

He carried the cooler bag out to the picnic area where the

guys and the two pretty women waited. Kelcie was tapping away on her phone, smiling in a way that made him wonder if she was texting with a man. Aiden was also on his phone, but he scowled and dialed.

"Jennifer, I don't care about what Roger said, you need to make the trade," he ordered, sounding irritated. Aiden looked up and, when he noticed Miles, pointed at Thomas then the basket and gave him a thumbs-up before turning away and moving off into the timber.

Not for the first time, he wished this picnic spot didn't have phone service. In the past, it had worked to their advantage. Today, however, was not one of those days.

After making sure Thomas got his favorite peanut butter and grape jelly sandwich with no crust, cut-up strawberries and Goldfish crackers, he gave everyone else their specialty Italian subs that he'd put together that morning while packing for the trip.

To her credit, Scarlett was the first to take a bite. She nodded in appreciation. Aiden looked at the ciabatta bread that Miles had picked up at the bakery before the sun had even risen with disdain.

"The sandwiches are freshly made and have a variety of meats including mortadella, capicola, *soppressata*, prosciutto and Genoa salami, provolone and a nice tapenade spread," he said, anxious that his guests enjoy the meal he had put effort into creating. "If the muffuletta sandwich isn't something you are interested in, I always keep a vegetarian charcuterie plate."

Scarlett leaned over to her friend and whispered behind her hand, "And I was worried about not having a chef. All we need is wine and it's like we are back in Italy."

He hadn't packed wine, but he smiled widely as he reached into the bag and pulled out sparkling waters and handed them to each, with the exception of the chocolate milk he'd handed to his little buddy. It wasn't the first time someone had complimented his cooking, or sandwich making as it was, but it was the first time it came from someone as sexy as Scarlett Leafletter. Something like that should qualify for placement on his résumé.

Thomas happily munched away, but his father wrapped the sandwich in his napkin and walked off into the meadow. A few minutes later, he spotted him throwing the perfectly good food into the timber.

After everyone finished eating, and Aiden loudly argued with someone on the phone about what sounded like stocks, he packed up the picnic supplies. He carried the bag of garbage over to where the horses waited and undid the straps on his saddlebag. The stupid trail cameras were still where they had been, and he didn't know why he hoped for anything different—of course, they wouldn't have gone anywhere.

He tried not to think of Chloe and Drake as he lifted open the leather flap on the bag. As he did, Seagrass nuzzled his neck with her nose, and when he ignored her, she opened her mouth and moved to nip his shoulder. He pushed her away. "You know better. Don't you think you're going to get away with that, Seagrass."

She shook her head, her dark mane flying with attitude. It made him chuckle, but the horse really couldn't get away with that kind of behavior if they were going to keep her around the kids. The last thing he wanted was for a kid to get bitten. He'd have to reevaluate her for guests. For right now, she was being precocious, but that could have been rubbing off on her from her rider.

He tried not to stare as Scarlett bent over and said something to Thomas. He handed her a wilted lupine and she smiled as she put it behind her ear. She was still out of Miles's league, but the way she dealt with Thomas made her seem more approachable.

She smiled widely as she stood up and patted Thomas's head. The action seemed a little forced, but endearing as Thomas reached into his pocket. In the center of his starfish hand was a coiled little ball. From far away he wasn't quite sure what the black thing was until it started to writhe and slither up the boy's arm.

Scarlett squealed and jumped back, covering her mouth with her hands.

He tipped his head back in a laugh.

Thomas squatted down and let the snake go, and it slithered happily off into the grass. The boy turned to Scarlett and put his hands on her arms and pulled her hands down from her face. Miles could hear Thomas trying to comfort her.

The terror on the city girl's face was cute as all get-out.

He walked back to the group, picked up the red-checkered blanket and shook it out. Scarlett grabbed the bottom corners and brought them over to him, helping him fold as he silently chastised himself. "What is the plan? Am I still in the back of the group?"

He laughed. "Yeah. I wanted to keep the Sullivans at the front. We don't want any more surprise garter snakes," he said with a laugh.

Kelcie looked back at her friend and frowned, as if asking if she was okay. Scarlett gave her an almost imperceptible nod.

"You have a good friend there," he said, nudging his chin in Kelcie's direction. "How did you meet your girlfriend?"

"We've been friends for a long time, then I hired her as my assistant. I needed the help, and she needed a job. I knew we could travel well together—two birds, one stone kind of a thing."

"So, you two aren't a *thing*?" he asked.

"No." She shook her head as she looked up at him, seeming to laugh at the idea and how far off the mark he was. There was something in her eyes that he couldn't quite make sense of, but he begged it was that she was attracted to him.

To hope for something like that was silly. "How did you guys meet?"

She lifted the other edge of the blanket and their fingers grazed against each other's. Her skin was so soft, but she didn't seem to notice the touch at all. He told himself to ignore the sensation of disappointment that moved through him.

"We met when I moved to Hollywood. Her father worked in Burbank. We ended up becoming roommates while we both tried to break into acting," she said, smiling at the memory as they walked toward the horses. "I made it, and she decided it wasn't for her but liked the lifestyle. Now, she's trying to break into screenwriting. She is really talented. She just got done writing a Western, based on…" She paused, as she let him help her up into the saddle. "Well, something like this, but in the 1800s. It's super good. I have my fingers crossed."

He opened his mouth to speak then promptly closed it. There were so many things he wanted to say, but all he could think about was the firmness of her calf where he had touched her through the fabric of her jeans. Every part of this woman was perfect. "I'm not sure exactly what it takes for her to get picked up, but if you say she's talented, I believe you."

Her face fell. "It can be very dog-eat-dog."

"We live in very different worlds, but some parts of life are the same everywhere you go."

He moved to Kelcie and helped her up and then the Sullivans, making sure everyone had their helmets strapped tight. Aiden was still on his cell phone and Miles had to tap him on the arm and give him the cut-it-off signal. The guy rolled his eyes, so Miles tried to mime that they would be losing service around the next bend. He felt ridiculous with his hand signals, but Aiden seemed to have put it together and ended the call.

After getting everyone moving down the trail, Miles got into the saddle and moved after the group. His mind turned toward their conversation. She hadn't said she was exactly single, but he didn't get the impression she was in a relationship. As far as he was concerned, the playing field was wide open for a pass—if she hadn't been a guest.

As for her dog-eat-dog comment, there had been a darkness in her tone that made him sense there were things to unpack from within that sentiment. No one said something like that without having been hurt, and hurt badly. He didn't mind baggage, though—he certainly had enough of his own. His baggage had even texted him today.

He nudged his horse to a trot, not wanting to be left to his own thoughts. It didn't take long to catch up, and they rode in silence on the trail for the next mile. He was glad after the inane chatter of Aiden's phone call that had effectively ruined the tranquility of the picturesque meadow.

He wondered how often the man missed the moments of true living with his son by being on his phone and working. Though Miles could understand the needs of a job, he had a hard time watching workaholics fail to enjoy the adventures they worked so hard to afford and provide for their child. He could only imagine how hard it must have been when Aiden had lost his wife, Catherine, last fall to cancer. Miles had met the woman a couple of times and she had been so sweet and kind, and Thomas had taken after her. Perhaps that was what Aiden was really running away from.

Seagrass shuffled in front of him and tried to push past Kelcie and her horse, Oreo, while Scarlett was only half paying attention. Kelcie's horse slowed, and as it did, Seagrass lifted her head and took her chance, landing a bite squarely on the mare's gray haunch.

Kelcie's horse lurched forward with a painful squeal. It bucked. The paint's back rose like an arch and all four feet left the ground. Oreo's hooves hit hard, jarring Kelcie and forcing her sideways in the saddle.

Oreo bucked again.

Kelcie let go of the leather reins and reached for the pommel, but as she moved the horse spun and kicked, sending Kelcie right as the horse went left. For a moment, it looked as though Kelcie was flying, except her right foot was still holding strong in the stirrup.

"Whoa, buddy!" Miles called the mare, kicking his horse forward and moving toward the horse in an attempt to gain control over the situation.

Kelcie landed in the dirt with a *whump*, and the mare started to run, dragging her by her right foot. Her helmeted head bounced on the ground until Kelcie lifted it and curled her body upward.

"Dammit! Whoa!" Miles yelled, racing over to the mare and grabbing the reins. He pulled hard against them, jerking the horse and his to a full stop.

Blood poured from Kelcie's mouth and nose. Her eyes were wide with fear as she struggled to breathe. Tears rolled down her cheeks as she looked at Scarlett.

"It's going to be okay, Kelcie. You just need to remain still." He tried to calm her as he reached for his phone.

Then he remembered they were out of contact right at the moment her life was on the line.

Chapter Five

"I am so sorry," Miles said, making sure Kelcie was safely seated in Oreo's saddle after the horse had calmed. Her arm was up in a makeshift sling made from his black bandana, and he hadn't dared to pull her right foot out of her boot. That could wait until they were in the emergency room.

In his days at the ranch, he'd seen that kind of injury a time or two and it never turned out pretty. At the very least, she'd sprained her ankle, but at least there wasn't any visible blood coming from her hip or leg. She'd not torn any muscles at least that he could tell. One of his rodeo buddies had gotten caught in a stirrup and torn his hamstring so badly that it took surgery and months of physical therapy before he was supposed to be back in the saddle again.

Of course, his friend had been back in the saddle in less than four weeks, but what the doctors hadn't known hadn't hurt them. The requirements of life were therapy for the working man—it was how cowboys were made.

He and Scarlett had been doing well together, but now she was scowling at him. Of course, she would be furious. He'd told her the horse was a biter, and she'd even questioned Seagrass being in the back—she was a horse that needed to be in the lead, and even Scarlett had known it.

Miles made a mistake, and he had been the one to cause this disaster. Now, he was going to have to turn the entire group around and head back to the ranch. The Sullivans, well, Aiden to be exact, were the type who would ask for a refund because they hadn't reached the promised destination—regardless of the circumstances. Cameron Trapper was going to be upset. JMac Equine Therapy and guest rides were their new business endeavors, and the insurance costs had been through the roof. With this accident and the resulting claims, their premiums were going to skyrocket.

That was all without mentioning the fact he'd been hoping to bring on the rest of his family to the ranch as staff members to help wherever they were needed. His brother Jackson was already at the ranch, but the rest needed jobs, and with the economic situation in Montana being what it was—where even minimum-paying jobs were hard to find and housing costs running at a premium—the West Glacier Ranch was their best option.

This guide service had been his idea. He had a lot riding on this, and he'd already screwed up…royally. Not only were his other brothers not going to be hired, but he was going to be out on his butt.

Kelcie shifted in the saddle as she readjusted the bandana on her arm. She winced in pain as she moved. It was going to be one heck of a long ride out for her. "Are you sure you are up to riding?" he asked.

She nodded, her split lip puffy, and there was a crust of blood from her bloody nose. "What do they say? 'You have to get back on the horse'?" Her black helmet was gray with dirt and dust from her unexpected ride on the bucking bronc.

"I'm impressed that you're so willing, but if you're hurting, I can get a UTV up here or call in a helo to life flight you to the hospital. You don't have to tough it out. It's important to me, and my employers at the West Glacier Ranch, that you get out safely and—in this situation—avoid further injury." His voice wavered slightly as he said employers, unwillingly giving away some of his unspoken fears. He hated it, but there was no hiding his misstep, there was only hoping Scarlett hadn't heard his falter.

Kelcie waved him off as Scarlett rode up to her side.

"Look, Miles," Scarlett said, almost hissing his name. "Why don't you just run along with the Sullivans. Kelcie and I don't need you. I've seen this kind of injury before on set. There's no TBI and the pain is under control. I can get us back to the ranch and my car is there. I can take her to Logan Hospital in Kalispell to get checked out. And don't worry, we won't tell the Trappers a thing."

He glanced back at the family. The duo was standing at the edge of the trail. Aiden had his arms crossed over his chest and looked pissed off that his vacation had been interrupted. Thomas was shaking his head and tears were running down his cheeks. "Let me talk to them and see what they want to do."

"We'll just start heading back." Scarlett motioned toward the ranch. "You'll know where to find us." She turned Seagrass and nudged her forward, making sure to take the lead.

Kelcie gave him a stiff nod. "See ya."

"Again, sorry about what happened." He felt ridiculous apologizing repeatedly, but there was no other move in his cache. He could only repent. The beautiful woman he'd been making progress with was furious, and rightly so, he was quite possibly on the brink of losing his newly acquired role at the ranch, and he may have also cost his family their potential careers. No biggie—he'd just taken his whole family down in one fell swoop.

Nice job, jackass, he silently chastised himself.

He desperately wanted to jump on his horse and go back with the two women, but he was torn. He didn't want to tell

Jamie Trapper that he'd failed in his role with JMac and in helping Thomas deal with his past trauma—if anything, he had only worsened the boy's anxiety. He needed the family—and specifically Thomas—to continue.

Picking up his phone, he searched for service, but without going a mile back down the trail and risking coming out with the Sullivan family in the dark, he was stuck trusting that Scarlett and Kelcie could find their way safely back. As soon as he hit service again, he'd let Jackson know they were on the way and to keep a lookout.

As he watched Scarlett lead Kelcie away, he held no doubts that Scarlett was the kind who had led herself out of harder situations than this before. She seemed like she could deal with anything life could throw in her way. She also seemed to know horses. The bite and the rodeo had been on his shoulders—if he hadn't distracted her, the bite wouldn't have happened.

He walked over to the family. Thomas's eyes were puffy from crying. "Mr. Miles, can we please keep going? I don't want to go back. Daddy says we have to go back."

"It is up to you guys what you wish to do. The ladies are headed to the ranch, but I'm willing to continue our ride as planned just for you, bud. Let's ask Dad." He looked up from Thomas to Aiden. He didn't want to appear as though he was seeking absolution or pity, but as his nerves rose into his throat, he found that he sought both. So much rode on Aiden's decision. Cameron and Jamie would be furious if he failed to help the boy and if this incident hurt their growing business.

"Daddy, *please*," Thomas pleaded.

"Things should go smoother," Miles promised with a smile. "I have a stop at a private lake planned. I packed some rods to fish. You guys will love it when we get some trout in our hands."

Aiden had been mollified. "Okay. Let's go." He looked at Miles with a scowl. "No more accidents, hear me? If another thing goes wrong, not only will we not be paying, but your new ranch will be getting a horrible review and you'll be hearing from my attorney."

"Mr. Sullivan, we've worked together in the past, and I'd hate for one little mishap to tarnish this new opportunity for Thomas to heal. Jamie's team of counselors are some of the best, and the horses are well...*horses*." Miles nodded, but his stomach lurched. He was playing with fire. "That being said, I always do my best to make sure everyone stays safe."

Promising safety was like promising love. A person could have the best intentions, but only time could reveal if the fates would play wicked or wild.

IT HADN'T TAKEN Scarlett and Kelcie long to get down off the mountain at Scarlett's preferred trotting speed. Kelcie hadn't seemed to mind the jostling, though Scarlett had kept asking if she needed to slow down—no doubt, Kelcie had wanted to get down the mountain and off the horse far more than Scarlett.

She should never have come back to the ranch. From the moment she had bought the airline ticket online, Scarlett had known this trip would be a disaster. Her brothers and sister hadn't seen her in years, and thanks to their narcissistic father and his golden-child system of parenting—wherein only one of them could ever be loved at a time and the rest were found lacking—it was unlikely she would have been met with open arms. That was, *if* she had told them she was coming. As it was, she was glad she had kept her family and their staff in the dark about her arrival. As it stood, she could simply slip out just as quickly as she had crept onto the ranch.

The only problem was, she didn't know where else to go.

Butch was still out there and looking for her. This was the last place he would think of looking for her—he knew how much she hated this place and how much she had hated her father.

Then again, he also knew her father had been killed. Yet, there was nothing here that would have drawn her back. They had talked about it a few months before everything had blown up in the headlines of the small town of West Glacier.

Butch had loved to make fun of her melodrama of a life back in "Hicksville," as he called it. He wasn't wrong in some ways—it was a little backwoods—but at the same time it was its antiquated ways and old-world manners which imbued it with its certain charm. When she had driven to the ranch from the airport, when she'd gotten off the highway and onto the smaller roads, people still did the two-finger wave as they passed. At the gas station, where she had stopped for a terrible burnt cup of cheap coffee and to freshen up, the cashier had recognized her as being from out of town and had started a full ten-minute conversation about California.

It was a well-known fact native Montanans didn't like Californians, and there were bumper stickers on many cars that read No Vacancy with the Montana state outline. But when people spoke face-to-face, it was rare that folks were anything other than cordial and welcoming. In fact, in the case of the gas station attendant, Jose, they were almost a little too welcoming. They hadn't seemed to pick up on her body language cues that she had wanted to leave and *really* didn't want to make small talk about "home."

If she had told Jose the truth, that she was one of the long-lost Trapper daughters, the secret would have spread like wildfire through the prairie and her family would have known she was back before her tires touched the ranch's dirt access road.

Things could work to her benefit like that here, too. If she wanted to know gossip about someone, all she had to do was ask the right person and she could find out just about anything she wanted to know. Hair salons, bars and churches were the best places to go for the full gamut of dirt. Nothing ever stayed a secret in a place like this for long, unless a person was the only one to know.

She glanced over at Kelcie. Her assistant knew her secrets, but Scarlett wasn't worried. It wasn't as if Kelcie was from here or talking to anyone in this small town. She knew the rules of her position and she had signed the nondisclosure agreement when she took her job. It all came with the territory of working in Hollywood and film. There were more secrets and skeletons in the business than there were buried under the city of Savannah.

As they arrived back at the ranch, there was another hand standing outside the barn, a man she didn't recognize. He had dark black hair and looked like he was in his midtwenties. He wasn't bad looking, but nothing compared to Miles.

It was good she was leaving the ranch. She had no business being around a man like Miles. He was far too good-looking and the man most likely to next break her heart.

A man who spent his days breaking horses and pleasing guests, well…he would probably know exactly how to run her heart directly into the dirt in the corral near her family's barn.

The cowboy walked over and took hold of the reins of Kelcie's horse. "What are you guys doing back? Where's Miles?" he asked, his voice raspy. He smelled strongly of leather conditioner and hay.

"He stayed up on the trail with the other guests," Scarlett said, speaking over Kelcie, but sending her a smile to try and make up for her rudeness. "My friend had a bit of a bronc situation with her mare here, and we are going to need to run to Logan and get a few X-rays."

"Oh," the man said, glancing to the handkerchief sling and then instinctively down at her leg and stirrups as though he knew only too well what kind of injuries occurred when a horse went wild. "I'm sorry to hear you had problems on the mountain. I would have come up and helped you back had I known you needed anything." He held out his hand. "By the way, I'm Jackson Miller."

"Are you Miles's brother?" Kelcie asked, sounding just a touch too drooly.

"Why, yes, ma'am, I am." He gave her an over-the-top tip of his white cowboy hat.

The action almost made Scarlett laugh at its touch of unctuousness, but Kelcie let out a schoolgirl giggle.

Scarlett wanted to smack her gently to pull her back into reality and away from whatever fantasy she was having about the admittedly handsome cowboy right now. Then again, if she did, she would be some kind of hypocrite when she had been doing the same up on the mountain about the man's brother.

What was it about this family that brought on the swoon factor? Maybe they were the ones who should have been in Hollywood.

For a moment, she envisioned walking onto the red carpet for her next premiere with Miles on her arm. He was wearing a black suit, black shirt, bolo tie and a white hat like his brother's. Every woman in the entire state of California, not to mention the rest of the world, would stop in their tracks. She would be the envy of them all.

And yet, he was nothing but trouble.

"We need to go," she said, pulling herself back to reality.

Kelcie shot her a look, as though she had momentarily forgotten her pain—that was until Scarlett silently noted her arm and ankle. Kelcie sighed and her body sank deep into the saddle. The mare under her dropped into her haunches as her rider moved, following her lead.

"I don't know what happened on the hill," Jackson said, "but your horse seems to like you. You will need to come back when you are done at Logan and visit her." He sent Kelcie a spicy smile as he wrapped the reins around the hitching post and then helped her down out of her saddle.

Kelcie limped on her ankle, her face contorted with pain, but she tried to control it as he helped her over to the wooden and cast-iron bench on the other side of the sliding doors of the barn. She had her arm over his neck and was leaning into his body, and as Scarlett watched a strange wave of jealousy washed over her. On the other hand, she was happy for her friend. It had been a long time since Kelcie had dated anyone. In fact, she couldn't remember anyone serious in her life for the last few years. Lately, it had only been one-night stands or situationships with other people on sets.

It seemed like everything Kelcie did was in line with their lifestyle.

They both sacrificed a lot for this job. If Kelcie wanted to go heart-eyed for this cowboy, she would have to be supportive. Her only fear was that she would get hurt, but if she did, Scarlett would be there to help pick up the pieces. It was the least she could do.

As Kelcie and Jackson talked about what had happened on the mountain, Scarlett climbed down off Seagrass and looped her reins around the post. She didn't fail to notice that Jackson had completely forgotten there was another guest to take care of, but instead of being upset she found it sublimely cute, albeit with a side of the green monster.

If only they hadn't had issues on the mountain, she could have lived out her fantasy of being a cowgirl high in the backcountry with a handsome cowboy she barely knew and may never see again. Oh, where could things have gone.

She ran her hand down Seagrass's neck and cooed her thanks to the beautiful mare as she loosened up the girl's saddle. She moved to Kelcie's horse and followed suit.

Jackson was busy taking off Kelcie's boot, and from the look on his face, her ankle was going to need attention. He turned to her. "I know you said you would take your friend here to the hospital, but I wouldn't mind running her in for you. I know the roads inside and out and I can get there quickly. How 'bout I take her? Or, we can all go together?"

She wasn't about to go and rain on Kelcie's parade, and she didn't want to tell the man she probably knew the roads just as well as he did, so she simply shook her head. As much as she didn't want to stand around and wait on the ranch for her friend to return, she wasn't about to block her friend from spending a few hours with the man who would undoubtedly be the focal point of her upcoming fantasies—and potential reality.

The lucky woman.

Kelcie, who must have picked up on her conundrum, turned and put her hand on Jackson's chest. "Is there a guesthouse or somewhere that we can rent for the night? Somewhere that Scarlett can put her things down and get some rest while she waits for us? We hadn't gotten a hotel around here yet, and I'm sure she could use some downtime."

Oh, how she loved her friend. Especially when she understood and appreciated her need to hide.

"I would say you could have my place, but I have a crummy apartment, and you wouldn't want to stay there—it's not up to your standards, I'm sure." Jackson sent them an apologetic glance. "However, they have guest cabins here, and I can get you set up in one of them."

"That would be great," Kelcie said, limping behind Jackson as he moved toward the small shed-style building that acted as the guest services area.

"There's a really nice cabin, the Saint Ignatius. It's right down by the river and it has a porch where you can sit on the swing and watch the river go by. It's awesome, I just need to make sure it's available. It's normally only for our VIP guests, so it'd be perfect for you. To be honest, I'm surprised you don't already have it booked." Jackson opened the door and walked inside the office building. He clicked away on the computer. "It looks like it's open, and I can give you a free night tonight because of what happened on the mountain, and a great rate if you guys want to stay longer."

"We're not staying for free," Scarlett said, taking out her phone and pulling up her digital wallet. Nothing in this life was free, and she didn't want to owe her family anything if they found out who she really was. "Charge us the going rate. I want to support the ranch."

"I'll talk to Miles when he comes out, but you won't be charged until the end of your stay. Do you know when you'd like to check out?" Jackson took her phone.

"I need to get back to work soon," she said, which wasn't entirely a lie, though she didn't have any concrete plans. "Let's say a week?"

"Done." He clicked on a few buttons, and she tapped her card.

As he handed back her phone, she motioned toward the horses, which were still tied up outside the barn. "If it's okay, I'd like to take care of them so you guys can get going. Is that okay?"

Kelcie shot her an appreciative smile.

Jackson chewed at the corner of his lip as if he was concerned about getting in trouble for shirking his duties if someone came out and saw a guest, alone, putting away the tack and brushing down the horses. "I don't know."

"Just go. No one has to know. And if they find out, I'm sure they'd understand the extenuating circumstances." Scarlett sent him a wilting smile.

Kelcie touched his arm and nodded in agreement. "Let's go, please."

It was the straw that broke the camel's back.

From the pale color of Kelcie's face as Jackson helped her into his pickup, Scarlett was glad he didn't resist her request to head out. Yet, as the sound of the truck and the crunch of its tires on the gravel road faded into the distance and was replaced with the quiet sounds of the ranch, a sense of fear and loneliness swept through her. For the first time since she'd arrived in Montana, she wasn't sure exactly what it was or why, but she felt truly vulnerable.

Chapter Six

Miles was exhausted as he made it back to the ranch, dropped off the Sullivans at their guest cabin, and rode back the mile or so to the barn. He spotted the starlet's white rented Mercedes-Benz in the parking area, and a lightning bolt of excitement buzzed through him. She hadn't hit the road—or maybe she had, and she had just abandoned her rental car there with the intention of having one of the ranch staff members return the car to the airport.

It wouldn't have been the first time an entitled guest had made an unusual request.

What was wrong with him? First he was glad to see her car and then he called her entitled.

He just couldn't decide how he really felt about the woman. There was something about Scarlett that had immediately rubbed him the wrong way, but there was also something so ethereally beautiful about her soul that he wanted to pull her into his arms and kiss her until he could understand every part of her being.

He thirsted for her in ways only a man who was dying of thirst on a desolate island could fully understand.

He was pathetic.

He'd only just met her.

There was no such thing as love at first sight. Lust, for sure, but love—no stinking way. Insta-love was for mushy, gushy date-night movies. Reality sucked. Love in real life was broken promises after years of dating and engagement, breakups and shattered hearts. For him, it was finding out he had been cheated on by way of an unlocked phone screen and one unforgettable naked man's picture.

If only he could burn that image from his mind.

He could have even believed his ex, Chloe, when she had tried to tell him the picture was unsolicited, but when he'd asked to see the rest of their communications and she had blanched, everything ended. He'd walked out of their apartment and never looked back.

Yeah, forget love. Forget lust. Forget women.

Then again, maybe Scarlett was different. She wasn't from here. Maybe in Hollywood they had come full circle and returned to the land of mutual respect and upheld promises.

All the women he'd ever been with had wanted him as their protector, and he'd happily taken the role, but losing Chloe had shaken his ability to feel up to the task in a romantic relationship. It wasn't that he was incapable of protecting them, it was just that in doing so, he risked losing himself and his heart. And now he had a sinking feeling Scarlett was looking at him in the same way.

Yet again, she had ridden away on the mountain after making a point of telling him they could make it out on their own—and thanks to the heavy prints in the dirt leading toward the barn, and the flurry of texts he'd received from Jackson about him running Kelcie to the hospital, it was safe to say Scarlett had been right.

As he pulled his horse to a halt and got off, hitching her to the post, Scarlett came prancing out of the barn. Her long hair was pulled up into the sexiest messy bun he'd ever seen in his real life. She looked like the starlet she was, and tonight she was playing the role of cowgirl.

He wanted to dislike her for it, and yet there was that damned draw to pull her into his arms. He focused on the freshly stitched brown leather cowboy boots on her feet, with the J toe. They had to be pinching the hell out of her toes and hurting the balls of her feet thanks to the long day of riding and their newness.

Maybe there was something to being broken by women—at least he had learned to protect himself thanks to his pain. If nothing else, the past hurt could help from encountering future agony. *If a guy was smart.*

"How's Kelcie doing?" he asked. "Jackson told me he ran her to the hospital to get checked out. Have you heard how it went?"

"Hello to you, too." She pushed a strand of hair out of her face. "I haven't heard a word from either of them since they left." She stopped beside him and waited for the horse to acknowledge her before she ran her hand down her neck.

"Sorry, didn't mean to be rude." He patted the horse. "You're good with animals."

She shrugged. "Apparently not good enough to stop Kelcie from getting hurt," she said, regret flecking her voice. "I can't believe I let Seagrass get away with that. You had even warned me." She let out a long huff.

He didn't want to tell her that it was more his fault. "Things happen on the trail. I'm just hoping Kelcie will be okay and that—"

"I don't *cause problems* for you." She didn't even blink as she finished his thought, as though litigiousness was so prevalent in her world that it was an everyday conversation piece.

"No," he argued, halfheartedly.

She stopped him with the raise of a finger. "It's fine. I already told you, I don't plan on pursuing any lawsuits, and I know Kelcie feels the same. She isn't one to make waves. If anything, I think she was glad to be with your brother." She sent him a coquettish smile that chipped away at the ice he'd tried to use to enshroud his heart.

"He's a good man. Smarter than he looks." He chuckled as he remembered his brother's party the night he had graduated from the University of Montana. "He has a degree he will likely never use in mathematics."

"He's a mathematician and he works as a ranch hand? How does that happen?"

He arched a brow as he picked up the judgment in her tone. "Can't smart people work on ranches?"

She opened her mouth, looking horrified, as she must have realized how she had sounded. "I'm sorry, I didn't mean it like that. Not at all. I'm just surprised he isn't working for a tech company or something." Her cheeks were flushed with embarrassment, and it made her look impossibly sexier.

"He could. He had job offers in other parts of the country, but he didn't want to leave Montana. After everyone went back to the office, his former job did, too and he wasn't willing to give up the West."

She looked at the snowcapped mountains that seemed to rest just at the edge of their fingertips in the sky. "That's something I can understand. Your home is beautiful. Leaving Montana is for the stupid." She smiled, but there was something in the way she looked back at him that made him wonder what he was missing. "Do you like your boss?"

"Mr. Trapper?"

"Isn't it Cameron?" she asked.

He nodded. "He and his new wife are great. Good to work for. He's always out doing something on the ranch, and he puts in as long, if not longer, hours than the rest of us."

Her phone rang, and a darkness cast over her features.

"Everything okay?"

She nodded, but she couldn't look him in the eyes as she silenced her phone and dropped it into her purse.

"You must have a ton going on in your life. You get a lot of calls. You working on a show or something?"

She gave a dry laugh. "Busy, yes. I have an upcoming project for a streaming service, but I'm looking for new roles. I'm trying to get myself into the right chairs, but I'm constantly finding them pulled out from under me."

"Nothing quite like landing square on your ass to reset your life's compass." As he spoke, she turned, and he couldn't tell whether or not he had plucked the right thread. "Is that what brought you here? Work troubles?"

"Something like that." Her phone buzzed from her purse, and she pulled it back out.

He tried to see who was calling, but as he stepped around her, all he saw was the black screen.

She turned back to him, appraising his closeness with a disapproving scowl. Instinctively, she placed her cell phone over her heart and away from his prying gaze. "Would you text Jackson? Kelcie isn't responding. I'm getting concerned. She's always on her phone."

He nodded as he pulled out his device and sent his older brother a message. It went unread, and, trying to call, it went straight to voicemail. Jackson wasn't great at the phone, but given the circumstances, there were only a few explanations as to why the two weren't answering.

For now, he had to hope it was that they were just busy with a doctor or nurses and held up from answering. The only other explanation was if they were doing something that Jackson had no business getting involved in when it came to a ranch guest.

Scarlett cleared her throat and pulled his attention to her

and the fact that if he was judging Jackson for going after the hot Hollywood girl, he was the pot calling the kettle black.

He lifted his phone in surrender. "I'm sure they will get back to us as soon as they can. They know we are waiting." He had to do something that would keep this woman at arm's length long enough for him to get his head clear, but not so far as to run into problems with Cameron. "When did you fly in? Have you had a chance to look around the area much?"

He felt stupid making small talk, but there was something in the way she looked at him that made him feel like he was back in high school, and he had no idea what step to take next. He hadn't dated since things had ended with Chloe, and his ineptitude was creeping up in his bones. It had been five years since he'd gone on his last first date.

It wasn't that he hadn't noticed women. There was one particularly good-looking thirtysomething who worked at the family-owned six-aisle grocery store a few miles from the ranch. For a man who didn't have to cook much, he was hitting the market far more often than most would have considered necessary. However, after a long day in which he'd only spoken to horses, sometimes it was nice to see a pretty woman who always met him with a warm welcome.

There wasn't anything there with her, once they went beyond pleasantries, but when loneliness crept in, he hadn't needed more. Truth be told, he wasn't even sure he would have been, or was, ready for anything beyond hello. Based on the way he was acting around Scarlett, he would be ready to date sometime around the next millennia.

"We just flew in and got the rental car." There was a strain in her tone that edged on reluctance, but he wasn't sure why or what she would have been hesitant to tell him.

Maybe he was just picking up on her concern for her friend. He couldn't begrudge her there.

Her phone pinged, and she took it out of her pocket.

"Kelcie?" he asked.

She shook her head as she let out an audible groan.

"Do you want me to answer it?"

She didn't seem to hear him as she looked at her phone. Some of the color bled from her face. Her hands began to shake.

He reached down and put his hand upon hers, drawing her attention back to him. "What's going on? Really."

She pulled her hand away from him, making sure to hide her phone's screen as she moved. "It doesn't matter."

Her phone buzzed again. She tilted her head back in exasperation, but instead of ignoring the annoyance, she turned around and pressed onto the screen. Her fake fingernails clicked hard on the screen as she typed away, and he could hear the fury in her harshness.

He had no idea what was going on, but the intensity of her rage pulsed off her and filled his soul.

This kind of reaction from a woman, especially one who didn't want to talk about it, could only mean one thing—she and her boyfriend were having a fight.

Chapter Seven

The messages on Scarlett's phone were breathtakingly simple, and heart-stoppingly short:

You think you are clever.

Thirty seconds later, she was hit with the next blow.

You can't get away from me.

Butch was baiting her. She had fallen for this trap and answered, afraid that he was telling the truth and forcing her to act, so many times in the past year it made her nauseous at the thought. He wanted her to answer. He was just bluffing. He had no idea where she was or what she was doing.

If she answered now, he would know he had gotten to her. This cat-and-mouse game would be intensified, and she would be pulled back into a text string that she didn't want to endure. No doubt if she did fall for it, he would end up telling her how much he loved her and then telling her how much she *loved him*, when in reality there was nothing about her former agent that she found attractive.

When he had first discovered her and pulled her up from the no-names to the silver screen, she had been so young, excited and naive that she had been his perfect victim—tailor-made to fall for his quick wit, his lies, his promises of grandeur and the false sense of security that came with being his "number one."

It hadn't started as anything—it was just a friendship, banter between colleagues. Looking back, what a fool she had been, but when an actor was young and hungry, the agent working for the talent was never supposed to be the one in the power position. They were to be a team, making money together, succeeding and moving her career in an upward direction.

If friendships transpired, so be it, but they weren't a regular occurrence and certainly not normal. It was more of a realtor-seller relationship. Civility, decorum, aplomb and grace were common—yet, when he had started texting her late into the evening and well into the night, she had thought he was just being a great agent. She hadn't seen it for what it really was.

She had been a fool.

Yet, when did flirting turn dangerous?

She had thought two adults could laugh and flirt without fear of stepping into the forbidden. Money, business and her continued growth as an actress were far more important than sex—he had to see that, too. Sex was easy, but they both needed each other to make a go of the dog-eat-dog world of Hollywood.

She had been wrong.

Her friend was someone she could trust. They'd been talking for a long time, and he'd never crossed the line. Usually, they discussed nothing beyond topics in line with their business, but then he'd go a little too far—telling her how beautiful she was, what a great actress she was and would continue to grow to be if she stayed close to him, and how if she just trusted him they would be a power couple.

Looking back, the trap she had fallen victim to had been so easy to see.

She had bought it all hook, line and sinker. She had been a sucker for his charms. Desperation had primed her for his grooming.

What she would give to go back in time.

That night when he'd followed her home, he had first tried to kiss her. She could remember it as if it was yesterday. She had been telling him about the producer who had gotten a little too handsy at dinner and how uncomfortable he had made her. In response, Butch had been telling her how sorry he was and how she hadn't deserved that kind of treatment.

Stories of slick-handed producers in the business were common, and she hadn't walked into the business completely unaware, but she'd never realized she had been standing in the fire and merely watching it cast off embers.

He'd come up behind her, asking to touch her. It had been strange, but he had touched an arm, laughing and grazing, the simple touches that were almost mindless. Then, he started to massage her shoulders. At the time, and slightly drunk, she'd yielded. Her brothers had massaged her shoulders, men could touch women without it being something more.

Oh, to have been twenty again.

She couldn't even blame the man—not completely. He'd asked to touch, she just hadn't understood what he had meant, and how the massage would turn to a hand over her shirt and against the soft cup of her bra.

She had pulled away. She had said no.

In that moment, he'd stopped. He backed away, moving to the couch near her and falling back. His eyes welled with tears, and he began to cry.

The emotion was so strange to her, a cowgirl in the big city, that she hadn't been able to comprehend the guy's reaction. She had said no—what was there to cry about? He had been the one to invade her space, to press the boundaries—and she had made him honor her wishes. If anyone should have been upset, it should have been her.

Eventually, he apologized and told her how sorry he was. Once again, she'd fallen for his game. Yes, she'd screwed up. She was the one who had allowed him back in her suite.

He had been in her room before. Yet nothing had ever happened.

She must have been sending off signals. It had to have been her fault. It always took two people. Maybe she hadn't made her line with him clear enough. Or, maybe, had she not spoken about her disinterest at all? Had she taken it for granted that the silent lines of business would keep his feelings in check?

It hadn't been that she didn't like him. No, she had. That was what had made it even more confusing. They were so close. It made sense that he had gotten the wrong signal.

Yet, when he'd finished apologizing and composing himself, she'd asked him to go back to his hotel. That was when things went from bad to worse. He'd barricaded the door. Refusing. He'd threatened her, her career, her life.

Her hands started to shake. Her phone and the messages were still glaring at her.

The phone rang.

She hit Ignore.

"Scarlett?" Miles said, pulling her back to where she stood and the reality outside of the black contraption in her hands, which acted as handcuffs and blinders instead of the amenity it had been supposed to be.

"Sorry."

"You don't need to apologize," he replied, frowning. "What are you fighting with him about?"

She jerked her head up and met his gaze. "What? How did you know?"

"No one reacts like that to a normal business call." He gave her a sweet, considerate look. "I know we've only met, but you can talk to me about this stuff. I have some experience when it comes to dating and breakups."

Oh. He had it all wrong, but she could understand how he could have made the assumption.

"I don't have a boyfriend. That's not it."

The tightness in his features seemed to dissipate ever so slightly. "Then who is it you're fighting with? Family?"

"No, not family." She jerked, and she instinctively glanced toward the ranch house. Thinking about family infighting, the last thing she needed to do was be spotted by one of her siblings. "If you don't mind, I'd like to freshen up. Jackson set me up in a cabin, but he didn't tell me which one or where it was located. If you'd point me in the right direction, I'd appreciate it."

His dark look returned, but he nodded. "You got it."

She hated the tone in his voice. It was so dry and crisp—like she had stepped on autumn leaves and everything they worked so hard to grow was now turning to dust beneath her feet.

In an attempt to make the look in his eyes disappear, she added, "And, as much as I don't want to be a pain, I could use some food." She sent him her best winning smile. "Your sandwich was great up on the mountain, and I'm starving."

He returned her smile with a guarded one of his own. "Glad you think so, Ms. Leafletter. I'll make sure you get something else to your liking."

Her chest ached at the sound of her formal name. She didn't like this game. But she had already been testing fate by standing out here and waiting for him as long as she had.

If her brother or sister saw her out here, they would have all kinds of questions for her that she wasn't ready to answer.

That was, if they didn't just kick her off the ranch. The last time she had seen any of them was the day she had left this damned place. She had told them where they could all go, and how she never wanted to see any one of them again. At the time, she thought she'd meant those words, but now she had come to realize that the one person she had always really hated was her father.

Oh, daddy issues rearing their lovely heads. Again.

It was no wonder she had gotten herself into this situation. If only she had been stronger. If only she hadn't tried to paddle in a pool where she should have been wearing a life jacket—or better yet, not even have jumped.

He walked her to her Mercedes-Benz. "Why don't we take your fancy little car here. I can just walk to the bunkhouse from there. It's not far."

"It was the only rental the place had left. I would have preferred something more suited to the dirt road, but c'est la vie." She put her hand up in resignation.

She took the keys from her jacket pocket and tossed them his way. He caught them in the air with a flourish of his hand and a triumphant smile that quickly disappeared as he looked at her and seemed to remember the tension that rested between them.

He walked to the passenger's door and opened it for her. Waiting for her to buckle, he closed the door, but not before she saw his gaze drift down to her breasts. She celebrated her small victory. He wanted her, even if he didn't want to admit it, and even if neither of them could act on their mutual desires.

At least he didn't know that she wanted him as much, if not more, than he appeared to want her.

She watched him walk around the front of the car, his jeans tight on his ass as he moved. For a moment, she caught herself wondering what kind of surprise he kept hidden beneath. If the rest of him was as great as she could already see, she would be in trouble if she ever got the chance to be with him.

The car dipped slightly as he got in. He smiled as he started the engine, and he looked around the auto, assessing it like it was a new horse he was looking to purchase.

"You approve?" she asked.

He gave a dip of the chin. "I like my truck, but this is a nice rig. Gotta say, though, you're right. It wouldn't do well around the ranch in the wintertime. The roads can get a little dicey. In fact, even now, with the back roads of the ranch being muddy from the spring rains, it may be better if we hit the main highway and come around the back instead of trying to get you in the usual way."

She thought about how many times, when she had been a kid, they had pulled her truck out of the knee-deep mud in the far pasture when she had been tasked with feeding the cows. Those were days she would be only too happy to never repeat. Apparently, some things on the ranch hadn't changed, even if they had been updating the place. "Do whatever you think is best. I'm just the passenger."

He sent her a questioning glance. "You hardly seem like the kind of woman who just goes along with the plan."

She cocked her head, trying to decide whether she should be offended or not. "What do you mean by that?"

He pulled her car out of the spot, and they made their way toward the highway. "Don't get me wrong or anything, but from the moment we left the ranch this morning, you've had your own way of doing things and you always make sure to put in your two cents."

Yep, she was offended. "I guess you must not be used to

women who are assertive." She could hear how she sounded, but she didn't care. If he wanted to say triggering things, he could deal with the bullet.

He let out a long exhale. "Don't be upset. Please. I was really trying to pay you a compliment. I like how you're not afraid to speak your mind."

She nodded but had the distinct feeling that was the last thing he'd intended. "I come by it naturally." She looked back at the ranch house as it faded into the distance. "My dad wasn't one to mince words, either."

There was the sound of sirens in the distance. As they neared the highway, there was smoke billowing up in front of them. It was hard to tell where exactly the smoke was coming from, the road or from the ranch behind it.

She twisted her hands together as she tried not to think the worst. Kelcie and Jackson still hadn't answered. What if the smoke was coming from an accident? What if something had gone wrong?

Miles's face darkened and he sped up. Neither spoke. He pulled out his phone and checked for messages, as though he'd had the same thought.

"I'm sure it's fine." She reached over and put her hand on his arm as he dropped his phone into his lap.

He was hot under her touch, and there was the gritty feeling of dried sweat on his skin. He put his hand on hers and gave it a friendly pat. "Yeah." His smile was forced, and as she dropped her hand from him, she couldn't help wondering if her touching him had been a terrible mistake.

She'd been trying to make them both feel better, and less on edge. Instead, the acrid smoke permeated the air in the car, and it mixed with the tension she felt and made a sickening feeling rise within her. She couldn't explain why, but something was wrong.

Perhaps it was in the way he'd only patted her hand, or maybe it was Kelcie being gone, or the unknown billowing before them.

They turned the corner leading directly to the highway. There, at the end of the driveway, was the black Jeep Grand Cherokee, with a rental car sticker in the window. It was on its roof, and one of its tires was gone, only shreds of rubber and metal bands still on the wheel.

On the ground around the upside-down car was a pool of glistening liquids, black and brown, mixing and swirling and reflecting the late afternoon sun.

There was a set of footprints where someone had gotten out of the passenger side of the car and walked through the oil. The prints were smeared, and there was a mark on the road, near the black marks left by skidding tires. In the median, there was a pair of women's boots sticking out above the edge of the concaved and grassy surface.

"No..." Miles whispered.

"Do you know whose car this is? It isn't Jackson's, is it?" she asked, panicked as they slowed to a stop. "That's not their car. It can't be."

He came to a full stop. There was a gray Hyundai pulled over to the side of the road, and a man was on the phone. He looked panic-stricken as he motioned wildly with his hands as he spoke.

The world stopped around her as panic moved through her. Kelcie may be pinned inside, hurting or worse.

She reached down to grab at the door handle to jump out of the car. She had to help them. She had to help her friend.

"That's not Jackson's car." Miles's voice sounded like it was coming through a tin can on a string.

She looked over to him. His face was emotionless. "Whose car is it?"

"It's the Sullivans' rental. I saw it parked outside their cabin when I dropped them off. They must have been coming over here for something. Do you see the little boy? Where's Thomas?"

The horror of what she was seeing spread out in front of her hit her with the pressure of a hurricane. She couldn't stay in the car. She had to act. She had a little boy's life to save.

Chapter Eight

Miles moved to the driver's side of the Jeep as he listened to the sirens that were moving steadily closer. When he approached the smashed-out window, he carefully picked his way through the shattered pieces of glass, which littered the ground like crushed ice.

There was blood on the roof of the car, and as Aiden came into view, he could see the man's eyes were closed and his head was cocked at a strange angle. Blood was dripping down his hairline and falling onto the black fabric ceiling of the car. He pressed his fingers to Aiden's neck, searching for a pulse. It was slow and nearly imperceptible.

If the ambulance didn't arrive soon, he doubted the man would survive.

He'd sent Scarlett to check on the people in the Hyundai in hopes to keep her away from any of the horrors he feared he would find inside this Jeep. She had argued but not put up as much of a fight as he had expected—she must have been as afraid of the possible carnage that came with this horrible of an accident.

Kneeling down, he checked the Jeep's back seat. Thomas was strapped into his red and blue Spiderman booster seat, and he was crying. As the little boy spotted him, his quiet sobs turned loud. "Miles! Help me." His face was red and puffy, and tears poured from his eyes and moved down his temples and into his hair.

"I got you, buddy. You're okay," he said, trying to sound calm and even as to not further scare the boy. "You are being really brave, Thomas. Do you know that?"

He didn't want to move the little boy, but he had to get him out of the car. Help was on the way, but with the way the boy's face was so red, he worried that if he didn't the boy would pass out.

Thomas hiccupped as he nodded. "Is Daddy okay?" he asked.

Miles glanced at the back window to keep the boy from knowing the fragility of his father's condition by looking at his face. The glass had blown out in the back, as well.

"Your dad's going to be okay and so will you, buddy." He did a visual assessment of the boy, as he had been trained at the ranch for emergencies. Glass chips were embedded in the boy's cheek. Thankfully, Thomas didn't seem to notice, and the shards looked to be only superficially lodged. They weren't even bleeding. "How's your neck feeling? Does it hurt at all?"

The little boy shook his head. "My shoulder hurts," he said, touching the seat belt that was across his chest and where he had likely taken most of the impact from the crash.

"Can you breathe okay?" he asked, pulling the knife he always carried out of his pocket and flipping it open. "Do you hurt anywhere else besides your shoulder?"

Thomas sucked in a big breath between hiccups but was stopped by a new spasm. However, he nodded. "I'm okay."

"Good, you're a good boy," he said, forcing a smile to help the boy feel more comfortable. "I'm going to cut your seat belt, okay?"

The boy nodded.

"You might slip down to the roof of the car. After you do, I need you to lay real still and I'll pull you out. Do you understand?"

"Yes, Mr. Miles." He sounded so tiny and frail that it tore at Miles's heart.

No kid should have ever been in an accident like this, but thankfully at least he was alive. He couldn't bear to think about what he would have felt if he had found Thomas in the same state as his father.

He lifted the knife for the boy to see. "Isn't this a cool knife?" he asked, trying to shift the boy's focus away from the pain he was likely about to feel when he released the restraint.

The boy stared at it as Miles reached toward him and pulled the strap just loose enough to slip the blade beneath. It sliced through the strap like it was warm butter. He held the strap tight as he dropped the knife on the ground and out of the way.

"Okay, buddy, I'm going to start letting you down. You ready?" he asked.

Thomas's eyes were wide with fear. It made Miles wonder how badly the boy was really hurt. Right now, the little dude was probably in such a state of shock that if he had sustained any injuries, he may not have been able to completely acknowledge them yet.

He'd have to be careful with the boy's neck. The last thing he wanted was to make the situation worse, or to further injure the child.

"I want you to keep your head and neck as still as you can, okay?"

The boy's eyes grew impossibly wider. "Why?"

"I think pretending is so fun," he lied. "I bet you do, too. So, I want you to pretend that you are like a big tree. Strong and straight."

Thomas's body stiffened against his hand where he held the belt tight.

"Good boy. You're doing such a good job." He smiled. "All right, here we go. You're like a big pine tree." He started to move the belt, loosening its hold on the boy, and he started to slip out of the Spiderman booster seat.

The boy smelled of urine and sweat, and he reached out and took hold of Miles as he got free of the seat completely. Miles slipped his arm under the boy and let go of the strap, holding the boy in place. "Here we go, my big pine tree." He reached in and took hold of the boy's legs. "Don't move your back." He eased him out of the car and maneuvered his tiny frame through the broken window, carefully avoiding the shards of glass that littered the edges.

Thomas moved into his chest, burying his face in his shirt. He could feel the hot wetness of his tears against his skin. "You're okay, buddy, you're okay," he cooed, trying to make the boy feel safe.

He looked back at Aiden, who was still unconscious in the front seat. The sirens were growing nearer. They'd be here within a few moments. As much as he wanted to help the older man, he held the boy tight. Thomas was the one awake and aware—he needed Miles more.

"The ambulance will be here in a second." Scarlett came running over. She looked as though she wanted to take Thomas into her arms but stopped herself. "The guy over there wants to know how Thomas is doing."

"He's good but going to need to see a doctor," he said, but he showed the man Thomas and glanced to the glass in the boy's cheek. "He is so strong and brave."

"Is Aiden okay?" She looked toward the Jeep.

Miles pulled Thomas in slightly tighter to his chest as if the action could guard the boy from the truth. "Aiden..." He paused, glancing down at the boy in his arms. He was already hurt enough—he didn't need to hear that his father was possibly dead. "I'm not quite sure." Making sure Thomas couldn't see, he gave her a slow shake of the head as he pursed his lips.

He glanced over at the Hyundai and the driver, who was still on the phone with 911. "Did he see what happened?"

"He said the Jeep was already on its roof when he got here, but it was still spinning." Scarlett nibbled at her lip. "He wasn't sure, but he thought he passed a truck with a dented-up grille on the front leaving the scene. Like I said, though, he wasn't sure."

"Thomas," he said, "do you know what happened?"

He looked up at him, tears streaming down his face. One of the pieces of glass had wedged loose and blood was starting to seep from the wound on his cheek.

"Is Daddy dead?" he asked, his voice quaking with fear and the seemingly infinite sadness of youth.

Miles's chest tightened and he didn't know what to say, so he said nothing. Instead he pointed in the direction of the red and blue lights that were permeating the gray dusk. "Look, here comes your ride. Are you ready?" he asked, but he didn't wait for Thomas to answer. "They're going to take you to the hospital. Doctors and nurses are going to check you out. I'll tell them all how brave you've been, but I want you to keep being super brave."

Thomas nodded.

The ambulance careened toward them, pulling to a stop. A woman jumped out of the passenger door and rushed toward him, carrying a large black bag full of medical supplies. "Hi, guys," she said, trying to sound calm, but her gaze kept moving to the car on the ground. "My name is Becky and I'm here to help you. How are you doing?"

"Hi, Becky. I'm Miles, that's Scarlett, and this is the bravest kid I know, Thomas." Miles lifted him gently so the EMT could do a quick visual assessment. "I hope you don't mind. He was scared and upside down, so I pulled him from the vehicle."

"That's okay, Miles," she said, giving Thomas a wide smile. "I'm so glad to make a friend with such a cool kid! Will you be my friend, Thomas?"

He gave her a tiny nod.

"I bet that was super scary, but we're here to help. Can you be a big kid and keep being so brave while Miles carries you to the ambulance over there?" She pointed toward the vehicle. "There, I'll have him put you on a nice, comfy bed so we can check on your heart and your lungs to make sure they are all right, okay?"

Thomas looked up at him, questioningly.

"It's all right, bud. They just need to take you and your dad to the hospital. I'll get there as soon as you are taken care of and settled in."

The driver of the ambulance jumped out and opened the back doors of the ambulance. He grabbed his black bag, and the two EMS workers gave each other a knowing look. Miles had seen that look before. That was the look of resolve that came when people knew what they were about to encounter was going to leave behind a mark on the soul.

Chapter Nine

The world of one little boy was never going to be the same.

The evening air was pressing down, carrying darkness with it as Scarlett sat on the edge of the road next to Miles and watched as the wrecker arrived. Its yellow lights were streaking across the road and they cast an eerie shadow on Miles's face. She hated those lights, this place, the smell of death in the air and the horrific reality surrounding her.

Aiden was barely clinging to life, and from what she'd heard the first team of EMS workers say before they'd left, it sounded as though it was unlikely he would wake up. If he did, there was talk of severe traumatic brain injuries, but she didn't know how the workers would have known based on what they had seen.

Miles had been silent as they had watched the ambulance leave. He'd offered to go along but was turned away when Thomas had lost consciousness. She could still hear the wailing of the sirens as the ambulance had sped off toward Kalispell.

Hopefully Thomas would be all right and the EMS workers were wrong about his father. It wasn't fair that this little boy had to go through this kind of trauma so early in his life, especially so soon after he had lost his mom. No one deserved the hand life was dealing him, but least of all such an innocent boy.

As the police officer investigating the incident talked to the man who had been on the phone with 911, Scarlett overheard him saying something about another car, but she couldn't quite make out his words thanks to the ringing dissociation in her ears.

If they had been just a little bit quicker leaving the ranch, it could have been her clinging to life instead of Aiden. Or, it could have been Miles they raced to the hospital.

She looked over at him. His eyes were dark, and he looked somehow older than he had when she had met him that morning.

For a single day, it was one hell of a throwaway.

This one was definitely going to leave a mark.

The driver of the tow truck was taking notes beside the investigator, and he kept glancing over at them as if trying to get a read on how deeply they were involved with the accident and if they had something to hide. If only the things she was hiding were that two-dimensional—her secrets went far deeper and into a much darker past.

They had made their initial statements to the investigator, but he'd told them to wait for him to conclude his questioning in case he had any follow-ups. Right now, all she could think about was how sideways everything had gone. She'd come back to Montana to avoid death, and now the man she'd been riding the trail with only hours earlier clung to life.

Fate had a way of destroying even the most beautiful moments by reminding a person what evils lurked in the shadows—and she knew only too well how death watched and waited.

Miles reached over and put his hand on top of hers. As he did, she soaked in the warmth of his touch, but the weight of him pressed her hand into the gravel and glass on the side of the road. It dug into her skin, making pain spike up into her wrist and arm. She didn't pull away or even move. Sometimes pain had a way of pulling a person back to the present, and as badly as she didn't want to be there, she had things in her life that still needed to be seen to.

"Have you heard from Jackson?" she asked, looking at his fingers as he started to caress her hand and dig the detritus farther into her skin.

He shook his head. "Kelcie?"

"No." She motioned toward the detective. "Did he tell you anything about the truck? Did they look into the lead?"

He nodded. "I couldn't make out everything. But they are thinking it was some kind of hit-and-run."

She sighed. "Look at the Jeep… I'd say there's a damned good chance." She pointed toward the passenger side of the rig, where there was a concave mark as if the vehicle had taken an impact. There was black paint on the door from the collision.

"I hope they find the bastard responsible." Miles rubbed at a droplet of dried blood on his forearm.

"Do you think the deputy would be upset if we just left?" she asked.

Miles leaned back. "He knows the ranch. His boss is Cameron's wife, Emily. I have a feeling if he has a problem, he will know where to find us. If you want to go, I'll cover for you. You just go get in the car and I'll be right behind you."

She sighed, not really wanting to feel his touch disappear—it was the only thing in this moment that felt *warm*. His comfort was welcome, but she wasn't sure whether to trust the man who had literally ridden into her life on a beautiful horse.

Technically, she was the one who had come to him, but she wasn't about to argue with herself about the one thing that brought her comfort.

"I think we should run to the hospital. It's tearing at me

that Thomas has to face this alone." She looked in the direction the ambulance had disappeared. "Plus, maybe we can still catch Kelcie and Jackson. I can only think they are still there and that's why they haven't been getting in touch."

Even as she spoke, she could hear the feebleness in her words. The days of cell phones not working in hospitals were long passed. Kelcie knew how to get in touch with her. There had to be something wrong with her friend, but she couldn't handle the thought of one more thing going wrong.

THE HOSPITAL WAS busier than Miles would have expected when they pulled into the parking lot. The ambulance, the one he assumed had picked up Thomas and Aiden, was parked in the loop outside the emergency entrance, its engine running and its headlights shooting off into the distance and bouncing off the windows of the administrative offices across the street.

Miles hated hospitals. They reminded him far too much of all the things in his past and all the things he never wanted to think about in the future. In his world, hospitals only meant one thing—death.

In this case, in the life of the boy they had come to see, he had to hope this would be the one time death would wait. It had already come for the boy's mother—it could hold for Aiden.

Scarlett had been eerily quiet on their drive to the hospital, seemingly at odds with what they had experienced. If he had to guess, she had probably been wondering exactly why she and her assistant had come to Montana. It had seemed to be one heck of a cluster since the moment they had stepped foot on the ranch.

She had promised that they wouldn't cause issues for him or his employers, but he would understand if she changed her mind. In fact, he wouldn't be surprised if, as soon as she got a line on her assistant, she caught the next flight back to California. It would tell him exactly how close they were if she waited for Kelcie to get out of the hospital before she set to the air.

She'd been fighting with someone earlier. She'd said it wasn't her boyfriend, but dollars to donuts, that was the person and the reason she had run away to his neck of the world in search of reprieve. No matter how bad the scuffle, it couldn't have been bad enough to keep her from going back with things being as big a dumpster fire as they were.

"Do a loop through the parking lot. See if you can spot Jackson's pickup." She didn't ask and it should have rubbed him the wrong way, but he appreciated her taking control. In fact, he had been thinking the same thing.

They did a slow crawl through the lanes, but nowhere in the lot was his brother's beat-up Ford, the one he'd gotten after mowing lawns and doing maintenance at the local golf course for four summers during high school. Jackson had worked his butt off for that pickup, and with its one blue door on the gray rig, it was distinctive.

She was scanning the parking lot, her head on a swivel, and it reminded him of Emily, who worked for the local sheriff's department. She had the same way of constantly scanning wherever they were, as if she was always on high alert and expecting trouble.

Given the day they'd had, Scarlett's reaction wasn't a surprise, but it also wasn't a mannerism that was picked up by one crappy day.

"Did you ever play a cop?" he asked, trying to make a bit more sense of her.

She shook her head, but she had a thin smile as she thought. "No, I'm always cast as the thick-skinned businesswoman. Why?"

"No reason," he said, returning her smile. "You'd be good at playing one. I could see you being a badass detective or something. You'd definitely be the kind who wouldn't take any guff."

"That's why they put me in as the witchy woman." She laughed, but it carried a tone of a residual sting. "The last character I played was at least redeemable. Her name was Julie Crawflight—cosmonaut attorney and power-hungry social climber who was hell-bent on taking out her enemies. She was jumped after prosecuting a man who'd been arrested for killing his clan's leader. He was found guilty, but he was affiliated with the rival species, the Ragnons."

"Sci-fi and brawls, sounds like my kind of show. If there were naked chicks… I'm all over it." He laughed, but his mind went straight to her and how much he would give to see her without a stitch of clothing.

He felt his body stir with the thought.

"Oh, don't get ahead of yourself. It was just one season and hasn't aired yet. I'm supposed to start filming again in a few months, but that depends on—" She paused, looking away from him before seeming to collect her thoughts and planting a smile on her face that wasn't quite real. "It depends on a variety of things. This business is complicated."

"Did you get a copy of the show yet?" he asked.

She laughed. "Not yet, but I get to go to the screening soon."

"I'd like to see it. Maybe if you are taking auditions for a date, you'd let me give it a shot."

"It's not worth the minute to audition, trust me. Showings are so stressful." She sighed. "Truthfully, becoming an actress might be the worst thing that could have happened to me."

"I thought you said it was what gave you hope, empowered you?"

"And that, that right there is why it was the worst thing to happen. If I'd have just failed as an actress, I could have been justified in giving up and I'd have been forced to do something else. As it is, I keep pushing. I'm close to hitting it big, I can feel it, but then it seems like no matter how much success I attain, I'm still not getting to the levels I hoped for as a child. The best gift and the worst curse can be just that—hope."

"You're a dark horse, Scarlett."

"You have no idea." She pointed at a Ford pickup that looked similar to Jackson's. "Is that his?"

He shook his head. "They aren't here." He pulled into a spot by the doors leading into the entrance of the emergency room.

She made a strange sound as she sucked on her teeth. "I can't imagine where they are. I'm worried about them. Is this kind of thing, disappearing, normal for your brother?"

He shook his head before getting out of the car and walking around and opening her door for her. Jackson was many things, but unreliable wasn't one of them. If he gave his brother a task, it got done—no questions asked. He didn't want to tell her that he was more than concerned, but there was no denying that he was terrified about what could have happened to the duo.

They made their way into the emergency room in silence. The woman behind the desk was tapping away on the keyboard, and she didn't even look up as they approached the glass partition that kept them safely at arm's length.

After a couple of minutes of standing there in awkward silence and waiting for the woman as she sipped at her coffee, Scarlett said, "Excuse me?"

The woman finally looked up and seemed annoyed with their presence. "Can I help you?"

"We are here to see Thomas Sullivan. He came in via ambulance in the last hour."

The woman looked from Scarlett to him and to her computer. "Are you his parents or guardians?"

Miles shook his head. "Unfortunately not. They were involved in the accident as well. I'm not sure, but I believe the boy's father is already here."

The secretary nodded. "I'm sorry, if you aren't family we aren't allowed to have you back here."

"Can you tell us if any of the boy's other family is here? I'd hate to think Thomas is alone."

"His father is here and currently in critical condition. Thomas is considered stable. There're no other family members here. And that's all the information I can share with you at this time. If you'd like, when they are available and have been moved up to the floors, I can let them know you stopped by."

It made his hackles rise that he was being turned away from a child in need, but he'd known they were rolling the dice on getting through the doors to get by his side. "We are also hoping to check the status of her sister—Kelcie Sherry." He motioned toward Scarlett as the smooth lie melted off his tongue like butter.

"She was in a horse-riding accident this morning. Did she get moved up to the floor?" she asked, mimicking the woman's language.

The woman tapped away on the keyboard, but she sounded put out that they would have asked her for another second of her precious time. "How did you spell that last name?"

Scarlett spelled it out for her, but as she did the woman's scowl deepened.

"There doesn't appear to have been anyone here by that name. In fact, she's not even in our systems."

"What does that mean?" Scarlett asked.

The woman, whose name badge read Mary, finally looked up at them and met his gaze before looking toward Scarlett. "It means that she hasn't been seen here or any of the clinics associated with our hospital—that's any of the small walk-ins in the area. Are you sure she didn't go to Missoula to be seen?" If eye rolling could be heard in a tone of voice, it was in that exact moment even though the woman was keeping a professional stoicism on her tired features.

Scarlett looked toward Miles, her eyes wide with fear. He hated that look, but it echoed his deep unease.

"You know," the woman continued, "for this woman being your sister, I would think you would at least know what hospital she'd gone to. Some sister you must be. *Tsk.*" She gave her an appraising up-down glance. "I bet you're from California. Maybe it's best you just leave."

Scarlett lunged toward the counter and her mouth opened like she was ready to take a bite out of the woman, but Miles put his hand on her back and gave her a small shake of the head. This wasn't a fight they needed to have. The rude woman could wait. Right now, he couldn't explain it, but he had the feeling that his brother and Kelcie were in deep trouble, and if they didn't get more information—it would be them who would be the next to disappear.

Chapter Ten

It took Scarlett ten minutes to cool off and stop seeing red while they stood in the parking lot outside the emergency room. She couldn't believe the receptionist would have had the audacity to say a single thing about her level of care and consideration with Kelcie—regardless of the fact she really wasn't Scarlett's sister. The woman had been asking for a fight.

She was lucky she was behind a pane of glass, or Mary would have been picking bits of lip out of her teeth. It was personnel like her that gave hospital staffers bad names and reputations. Unfortunately, it seemed like in the last decade it was more common than not that Scarlett dealt with the Marys of the world rather than anyone else.

The crickets were chirping in the grass around the outside of the building, mixing with the sounds of cars passing on the road outside of Logan Health Medical Center. Scarlett hated the sounds of crickets. To some they were calming, even the harbingers of summer, but to her they were reminders of lonely nights and feelings of inadequacy. More, they were the sounds of agonizing loneliness. And for good or bad, they were the sounds of a sleeping ranch—without the bawling cattle.

Come to think of it, the sound of Mary's voice reminded

her of the latter. Maybe this entire state was one in the same as the ranch.

"I don't know about you, but I don't like the idea of Thomas being in there without someone he knows helping to get him settled in his room for the night. He must be so scared." She looked up at the mirrored windows of the second and third floors of the hospital. "I can't even begin to imagine what he is thinking. He came here to get over the loss of his mother and now this… The poor kid."

Miles put his arm around her, and there was such strength in his embrace that it reminded her that in this battle, she wasn't fighting alone. Thomas had both of them standing in his corner, and no matter what was to come, they would do whatever it took to help.

"Let's go find him." He gave her a searching look as he pushed down a flyaway hair.

She couldn't help the faint smile that took over her lips at the sweetness of his touch. "Unless you become a relative, I'm not sure how we are going to get in." She motioned toward her watch. "And now, it's after visiting hours."

He sent her a mischievous grin. "You know…you didn't seem to have a problem calling Kelcie your sister in there. Your acting could be just the key we need to get us into any door we need."

"Yeah, but my acting job is also the reason we were thrown out on our asses. She hated me and, for all we know, she lied about Kelcie and probably set security on us."

"You didn't like her, and she most definitely didn't end up liking you, but I didn't get the impression that she was lying. She wasn't screwing with us about Kelcie—she wanted us out of her hair. Sending us to her room would have been the quickest way to get rid of us."

The woman was a jerk, but she had at least given them

enough information to be reasonably sure Kelcie had never stepped foot in the hospital. Which left them with *nothing.* Which was perhaps why she was so angry. There were so many things happening, and all she wanted were answers but all she found were questions.

"We should have told her we were related to Thomas. That was stupid of me."

"No, you were worried about Kelcie, and you assumed the woman would be kind." He gave her a gentle squeeze before moving away. "Besides, you know there's more than one way to open a beer."

She cocked her head. "What in the hell is that supposed to mean?"

"It means that there's more than one way into this hospital and to Thomas." The mischievous grin returned. It made him look so handsome that her heart nearly stopped. "Your great acting skills are going to have to come back into play."

She shrugged. "I don't know about *great*, but…"

"Now isn't the time to be humble." He took her by the hand, and he pulled her in the direction of the main doors of the hospital that were a few hundred yards down the sidewalk from where they stood. "Just follow my lead."

An unexpected giggle rose from her, and its sound was so out of place that for a moment he paused and looked at her until she waved for him to keep moving forward. She didn't want to explain to him that it wasn't that she didn't take what they were doing seriously, it was just that any time she had to get into character, the first thing she had to do was get the nerves out—and in this case, it meant forgetting how handsome he was and how warm his hand was when it was wrapped around hers.

He laced their fingers together tighter as they walked around the side of the hospital and made their way into the front doors. There sat a college-aged young woman who had been tasked with working the night shift.

"Hi," he said, striding up to the front desk with a concerned look on his face that she forced herself to mirror.

The woman behind the desk looked up. At seeing them, her smile disappeared and turned to an expression of concern. "Good evening. How can I help you?"

"My name is Jim Sullivan and this is my wife. Our nephew was brought in here after a car accident tonight. Is there any possibility we can get his room number?"

"Of course," the young woman said, tapping on her keyboard. "What is your nephew's name?"

"Thomas," Scarlett added, her voice worn and tired. It felt wrong to be a fake family given everything the boy had been through, but if Thomas's mom was watching she hoped she knew that they were doing this to help comfort the little boy and be there in his time of need.

No child should have had to go through something like this alone. The thought had broken her heart since the moment she had seen Thomas whisked away in the ambulance.

Sure, there were nurses and hospital staff there to help attend to Thomas's needs, but when the thoughts of the accident crept into his mind, he needed someone there to hold his hand and be there emotionally.

As though his mother's spirit was there, Scarlett felt warmth on her forearm like someone had laid a hand upon her in reassurance. She didn't know why, but the strange sensation brought her a level of peace she hadn't realized she needed.

The front desk secretary looked up from her computer. "Your nephew has just been given a room in peds. It looks like he will be in room 316, but they are just moving him up from the Emergency Room. You're welcome to head that way. The elevators are just down the hall, or you can take the stairs, just there," she said, motioning toward the door just down the hall from they stood.

"Thank you, ma'am," Miles said, dipping his chin in appreciation.

Scarlett leaned into his arm, letting him support her as a mother would have given the weight of the situation they would have been facing if this really had been their son. He wrapped his arm around her and led her toward the elevators. They waited in silence until the doors slid open with a *ding*.

They stepped inside and hit the button for the third floor, and as the door closed, she eased out of his embrace. "Good job handling that," she said, smoothing her hair where it had been pressed against his chest. "I wasn't sure it was going to work, but I'm glad you got it done. I'm sure Thomas is going to be glad to see a familiar face."

"She was going to let us in, or I was going to have to go back to Ms. Mary and ask if she had ever seen a six-foot man come over a five-foot counter. There was no way I was going to leave Thomas."

She laughed, and the hollow sound bounced around the empty elevator like a loose basketball on an abandoned court.

Without thinking, she leaned into him again, and he put his arm back around her. Miles bent down, and she felt him kiss the top of her head. The feeling and the connection were so natural that she didn't question it. Instead she sank into the solace of the sensation of him.

The doors opened far too quickly, and he let go of her as they stepped out into a small pediatrics unit. It smelled of antiseptics, industrial cleaners and bland food, and the unit appeared to be made up of just two short hallways of rooms. Two nurses and a tech were making their way out to a far room and toward the stairs, talking animatedly. She caught them saying something about a car accident, but the door slammed as they made their way into the stairwell before she could make out anything else.

There was no one sitting at the main desk, and so they slipped past and made their way toward the room, and she peeked inside. Thomas was sitting in his hospital bed, looking wide-eyed around the room. He seemed stunned.

There was a nurse sitting beside him in a taupe vinyl chair, tapping away on a tablet, as she must have been asking him questions. Scarlett wasn't sure whether to interrupt, but when the nurse noticed her, she stood up and smiled. "Good evening. You must be Thomas's family."

Scarlett smiled, and before she could respond the nurse walked toward them.

"Thomas is just getting settled, but you are welcome to check on him. I can come back later to finish up my paperwork. If you have any questions or concerns about him, you're welcome to come chat with me when you are done talking." She moved past them, giving Miles a onceover and an approving nod before disappearing out in the hall.

The boy looked over at them and smiled widely. "Hi!" he said, sounding excited, but his voice was tired and worn as though he hadn't stopped talking since he had left them on the roadside.

"How're you feeling, kiddo?" Miles asked, as they made their way to the side of the bed.

Thomas shrugged. "My arm hurts," he said, lifting up a fresh cast on his right arm. It was bright blue, and it smelled like glue. "You have to sign it for me."

"You got it, buddy." Miles patted his leg.

"Did you see Daddy?"

Miles sent her a sideways look. "We didn't, but I'm sure you'll get to see your daddy soon, bud." He carefully stepped around the issue.

"Do you remember what happened?" Scarlett asked, wondering how much Thomas recalled seeing and whether or not the boy had an idea of what had truly taken place.

Thomas picked at his bottom lip. "I don't know. There was a big truck. Then there was a big *boom*. Everything went dark. I remember you guys on the road. I was coming here in the big 'bulance."

She smiled at the way he said the word in true five-year-old fashion.

"Did the big truck hit your car?" Miles asked.

Thomas nodded. "Santa was driving."

"Santa?" Scarlett asked.

He nodded again, still picking his lip. "He had gray hair and a big beard. He didn't have any elves with him, though."

Her stomach tightened. Butch had often been teased about his resemblance to the man in red. "What color was his truck?"

"Black."

"Did you tell the police about the truck, Thomas?" Miles asked.

Thomas nodded. "They saw my new cast, too." He smiled. "The policeman said he would sign it, too."

"I bet it's going to be covered in no time," Scarlett said, grinning.

There was a knock on the doorframe. "Excuse me." The nurse they had interrupted when they arrived was standing there, looking in on them. "I just received a call. Can you please step into the hallway so we can speak alone for a moment?" She had a look of grave concern on her face as she looked at them.

Miles turned to Thomas. "We will come back to see you, buddy." He walked over to the whiteboard on the wall and picked up the marker and wrote down his name and phone number. "If you need anything, you can have the nurses call this number. Okay?"

Thomas nodded. "Can you sign my cast before you go?" He pointed at the marker in his hand.

Miles clicked the lid back on the dry-erase marker before putting it back on the board. "Unfortunately, that one won't work, but I'll bring the right kind when I come back. Okay?"

Thomas looked crestfallen. "Okay."

"I promise we will. Right now, you need to get some sleep. It's well past your bedtime, lovey," Scarlett said, pushing back the boy's hair and moving it from his face. She leaned down and gave him a soft kiss to his forehead. "We'll be back to see you in no time. Again, if you need anything, we are here. And I know your daddy will be here to check on you as soon as he can."

The nurse cleared her throat.

Miles made his way out and Scarlett followed, giving Thomas one more quick wave before closing the door behind them. There was a large man dressed in black standing there, SECURITY emblazoned in yellow over the pocket on his jacket.

"David, our security guard over there, called," she said motioning toward the man. "It appears that they saw you trying to get through the Emergency Room entrance before falsifying information to gain access at the front desk." She sounded angry, but her voice and her face didn't match. "Since Thomas appears to know you, I told David we'll not be filing trespassing charges, however in the future I recommend that you do not try to gain access to minors through deception."

"How is his father doing?" Miles asked. "In all honesty, I'm a friend of the family. We were with them today on the mountain."

The nurse's expression softened, but only slightly. "Aiden

is awake, but he is going into surgery tonight. He broke his back in several places and has a fractured pelvis. He's likely going to have to stay in the hospital for some time."

"Does he remember anything about the accident, or the man who was behind the wheel of the other vehicle?"

The nurse shrugged. "That's something you'd have to talk to him directly about. *Tomorrow.*" She waved over to the security guard. "David, do you mind escorting them out?"

The security guard scowled as he stomped toward them.

"If anything happens in the night, we put our number on the board," Scarlett said, motioning toward the room. "We just want to know Thomas is safe."

Chapter Eleven

Safety was an illusion. Locks, cameras, seat belts…they all served good purposes, but they didn't stop people from getting hurt or bad people from doing bad things. Miles knew only too well how horrible people could be, especially when it came to getting what they wanted.

As they pulled onto the back road of the ranch and made their way toward the guesthouses, he couldn't help but wonder if they had skirted the line between good and bad in their attempt to gain access to Thomas. Even if their intentions were pure, their methods *were* a little questionable.

He recalled the expression of shock and fear on Scarlett's face when Thomas had told them about the man who had struck them. He wanted to ask her about it but was probably making something out of nothing. She wasn't from here, and it wasn't like she knew anyone in the area.

She had been strangely quiet ever since they had started back toward the ranch, though it was more than possible she was just as tired as him. It had been one hell of a long day.

They hadn't eaten in hours, and as he pulled up to the guest cabin his stomach gave a loud grumble.

She unbuckled her seat belt then turned to him. "Would you mind walking me in?"

The way she asked surprised him. It didn't sound like an invitation for sex—if anything it carried an air of fear. "I'd be more than happy. I know you're worried about Kelcie. If you want, I'll stay with you until we get a line on them. They have to be popping up anytime now."

"That's what you've been saying..." She gave an exasperated sigh as she opened the door of the Mercedes-Benz and stepped out.

She slammed the door shut behind her, not waiting for him to help her out.

This woman confused the heck out of him. One moment she wanted to be treated like a princess and protected, and the next she seemed to be pushing him away and resolved to take on the world alone. He wished she had come with instructions, or at the very least, that she would tell him exactly what she expected of him. If it was only a person to be by her side, it would be torture having to breathe in her sweet floral scent and know that he would never have a chance to kiss her soft pink lips, but at least he would understand the boundary lines.

As it stood now, all he wanted to do was take her inside and push her against the wall and kiss her until she couldn't speak and all she could do was moan for more.

His body stirred at the thought of the feeling of her soft lips on his.

She tapped on the passenger side window and pulled him from his fantasy. "Are you coming in?"

"Yep," he said, clearing his throat and forcing himself back to the reality that she was barely more than a stranger, a guest of the ranch, and utterly untouchable thanks to her celebrity status.

He followed her into the house, trying not to stare at the wide white stitching on the back pockets of her jeans. The round arc of her ass pressed hard against the fabric, making his mind drift back to the thoughts of pressing her against the wall.

She turned around as she got to the door, and she pointed toward the keypad. “Do you know the code?”

He walked up beside her, trying not to notice the way the breeze picked up the remnants of her flowery perfume, the hospital and horses on her skin. He pressed the numbers as she watched, and the door clicked open. He waved her forward and put his hand on her lower back as she stepped forward. She stopped for a split second, and she drew in a gasping breath as she tensed under his touch.

He dropped his hand.

He didn’t understand her reaction. What had happened between the hospital and now? She had eased into him in the elevator, even initiated the touch, but now…his touch was unwelcome?

It had been a mistake to touch her.

Clearly, she must have come to her senses and realized she was so far out of his league that it was like he was playing T-ball, and she was in the major leagues. If only he hadn’t let his daydreams get away with him, or if he hadn’t gotten caught up in watching those jeans move over the perfect round curves of her body.

He stepped into the house behind her and closed the door.

At least he had shot his shot.

And hey, she hadn’t slapped him or shut the door in his face.

Maybe there was some sliver of hope that there was a possibility for more between them.

Slipping off his boots, he made his way toward the kitchen in the large cabin. The place was huge, and it reminded him of what most people who came to Montana expected. It had an upstairs loft with two bedrooms and a bathroom, and a large bedroom, a kitchen and a living room on the main floor. Downstairs was a game room in a walk-out basement that led to a patio complete with an eight-person hot tub, which he often thought about sneaking over to use.

He'd never actually stayed in the cabin, but on occasions when the housekeepers needed help, he'd lend a hand in keeping the place. Once, earlier in the season, they'd had a family of six stay here and they had left one hell of a mess—even breaking one of the hickory dining chairs, which had cost more than five hundred dollars to replace. Until then, he wouldn't even have thought one of those monstrous chairs would have been possible to break without a jackhammer and a chisel, but three five-year-old triplets and a seven-year-old had managed to get it done.

That was to say nothing about the eggs that had been smeared all over the wall to the point that they'd been forced to repaint one area in the kitchen.

They had rapidly been added to the persona-non-grata list that started and ended with them.

Though he shouldn't have, as there was nothing particularly funny about what the family had done, he chuckled at the thought. Perhaps it was just the audacity and the lack of accountability and self-awareness that some people had when they stayed at places; it was as if they felt if they paid, they had the right to do whatever they wanted.

"You nervous?" Scarlett asked, dropping her coat and purse onto the edge of the chair in the living room.

"No. Just thinking," he said. "I hope you like the cabin. It's my favorite on the property. Honestly, I think it's even better than the main house. It's newer."

"I know. When was it built?" she asked.

He wasn't sure how she knew. It must have been on the website or something. She had already admitted she had done her research on the place. "It was just a year ago, or so. Before I came on. They've been renting it out as part of the new guest ranch endeavor. So far, it's been doing well. You have to come check out the view."

He moved to hold out his hand for her to take, but just as quickly dropped it, thinking about her earlier reaction. He didn't need her to kick him out of the house for real this time. He'd already pushed his luck further than he should have, especially considering that he was here simply to be a part of her guest experience and nothing more.

Though, admittedly, their guest experience was to have ended that morning. She was getting preferential treatment, but his bosses would have it no other way if they were to find out about everything that had happened.

He led the way to the stairs, and she followed him out to the back patio. There, babbling not ten feet away and down a set of steps, was the Flathead River. It was crystal blue in the lights cast by the house. The water moved slowly in this section of the river, but in the spring, it crept up the levee that had been built until it spilled over the opposite bank.

"The river comes out of Glacier National Park, so it's heavy with glacial till, or loam. It's basically the dirt that comes from the glaciers as they melt, and it erodes into the waters and runs out. There are certain areas in the park where the water actually looks milky white during certain times of the year thanks to the runoff. It's beautiful. You'll have to go with me to see it sometime."

He'd not intentionally offered her the invitation, but apparently, he couldn't help himself.

She gave him a sidelong glance. "Yeah, maybe I'd do that sometime. I've always wanted to visit Glacier during the runoff. I bet the flowers are amazing."

"The runoff up there doesn't happen until around early

June. Actually, they normally don't even have the roads completely open until late that month sometimes. You'd really have to stick around for the full summer if you wanted to appreciate all the park had to offer."

She smiled at him. "You know, one could say I'm here already." She stepped closer to him, and he caught the familiar scent of her. "That being said, I did miss the *spring* flowers."

He wasn't positive, but it felt like she was flirting with him. She must have been bored or something. There was no way she wanted him in the way he wanted her. She could do so much better than a guide working for a ranch. And it was just a few minutes ago that she had moved away from his touch. Seriously, she was so confusing.

She stepped closer to him and put her hand gently on his sternum. "Do you want a beer?"

He stared at her fingers and where they crumpled the soft flannel of his shirt and pressed into the hair at the center of his chest beneath. "Let's go grab a couple. We keep this cabin stocked for guests." His breath hitched in his throat. "There should be some steaks, too. I'll cook." His words came out staggered and airy as he spoke, but he tried to sound as cool, calm and collected as possible even though his heart was racing beneath her touch.

"I already told you that I wouldn't sue you for the accident today. You know you don't have to try to butter me up by making me dinner to keep me on your good side." She smiled, but her eyes were tired.

"Well, until we find my brother and your friend, I figure I must keep buttering you up. I may need to keep you deep in my pocket if Jackson decided to kidnap her, or something." He smirked as he tried to ignore the concern in his gut.

There was only so much they could do, and right now, for another twelve hours, they weren't considered missing persons, and they couldn't be reported to the police. Mary popped into his mind, and he groaned.

"Is that what my touch does to you?" Scarlett said, and she moved to pull her hand back, but he stopped her by pressing his hand over hers on his chest.

"No. That groan wasn't about you." He smiled. "I was just thinking about something else."

"If I'm touching you and you're thinking about something else, I'm not quite having the effect on you that I was hoping to have." She gave him a half grin that suggested she was fishing for a compliment.

"Oh, you're having more of an effect than you should be, trust me." He gave her hand a slight squeeze. "I'm just trying my damnedest to keep it professional. I have already been screwing things up right and left with you. I don't want to make things a thousand times worse by disappointing you, too."

"You think you'd disappoint me?"

He threw his head back in a laugh before catching her gaze. "A woman like you? I think I could keep you on your toes in bed, but what would you want with a cowboy? Our worlds are like comparing a longhorn to a lariat."

"I haven't heard that one before. Am I the longhorn or the lariat?" She laughed. "I'd prefer you didn't liken me to a cow."

He blushed. "Don't be twisting my words now, and don't change the subject. However, I would say you're the rope. You certainly have a way of tying me up in knots."

She stepped closer to him and moved up on her toes. His lips met hers. The kiss blindsided him in the most beautiful and seductive way, and in a way he'd never experienced before.

He'd been right about the knots.

She fingered the buttons on his shirt, loosening them and

letting his shirt fall open. She pulled it loose of his jeans. Before she could move lower, he pulled her close, hard against his body. His hand moved up in her hair, and his thumb moved against the soft skin of her face. He owned her with his mouth, kissing her in a way that spoke of how badly he wanted all of her.

She tasted like cinnamon and desire, a heady mix that made him hungry for more.

She moaned into his mouth, and he swallowed the sound like it was an appetizer for his soul.

He pulled at her shirt, loosening it from the back of her pants. She stepped back slightly, not enough to break their kiss, but just enough to be able to get to his silver belt buckle. She flipped it open and slid the leather strap loose, making his body instantly react. He ached for her.

He glanced at the hot tub that sat under the stars. There was a mink blanket folded and placed atop one of the Adirondack chairs. The last thing he wanted to do was break their kiss, but he brushed her cheek as he gently moved and touched his forehead to hers, looking her in the eyes. "Wait here a second."

He rushed to the blanket, but as he moved to grab it, he froze. Splattered across the surface of the hair was a dried blood-like substance. On the concrete, near the hot tub and around the chair was more dried blood. The chair had been scraped over the concrete, leaving behind splinters of wood, and droplets of blood had been spilled atop, plastering the splinters to the ground.

Something had happened here. Something bad. He looked for feathers or fur, in hopes what he had just found was nothing more than remnants of nature being its brutal self.

"What is it?" Scarlett asked.

"I'm not sure. Don't move, though." He put up his hand. "And don't touch anything for a minute."

She walked over to him. "Oh, my God. What happened? Is that from you?" She grabbed his arm and looked at it like she expected him to be cut, though the blood was already dry.

"That's not from me." He shook his head. "You and Kelcie hadn't been here yet, right?"

"No. Jackson just checked us into the cabin. He didn't even tell me where it was, he forgot in his hurry. That's why I had to wait for you."

That didn't mean that Kelcie and Jackson weren't there.

"Was Kelcie bleeding after the accident on the mountain? Do you think this could be from her?" He wasn't sure if he wanted the blood to be hers or just some stranger's. Either way, whatever they had walked into wasn't good.

"She wasn't actively bleeding, and certainly not enough to have left a trail like this if that's what you're getting at." She started to follow the trail. It led around the hot tub and up the hill to the main level of the house. She disappeared around the side of the cabin. "Come here. Look."

He followed, careful not to step in any of the droplets. As he came around the corner, he found bits of glittering glass strewn across the concrete outside the side door. The glass was shattered inward, where it appeared as though someone had punched in one of the glass panels of the door to get at the lock on the inside to let themselves in.

"We need to call the police," Miles said, slipping his phone out of his back pocket. "I'm sure they're going to be just thrilled to speak to me again today." He let out a long sigh.

He also needed to make the call he'd been putting off all day—to his boss, Jamie, who would undoubtedly need to chat with her husband, Pierce, and her brother Cameron about everything that had happened. His ass would be on the line and so would Jackson's. Everything he'd been working for would fall apart.

There would be no more hiding anything that had occurred, and all would be lost.

If anything, he feared he would be in even more of a pickle for not coming out and telling them about the kerfuffle that'd happened earlier in the day.

Before he could dial, Scarlett put her hand on his arm and stopped him. "Hold on, before you call. Let's take a look around. Maybe this was Kelcie and Jackson, and they didn't know the combination to the front door or something. I don't want to get anyone in trouble unnecessarily, if we don't have to."

There was a strange inflection in her voice, almost as if she was trying to hide something, but he feared calling the police and unleashing the events that loomed over his head. If he started asking questions about her tone, he might start pulling at strings he wasn't ready to pull.

"We won't touch anything," she said, pointing at the door. "Let's just go back the way we came. See if Kelcie was here. Maybe this isn't even from them, but if it is, for all we know, maybe they are in one of the bedrooms." She gave a forced chuckle. "If they are, you are the one who has to knock on the door."

"Deal," he said, hoping against all hopes that it was the case and the blood that was splattered on the ground wasn't an indication of something more ominous.

They made their way back around toward the hot tub as he buttoned his shirt back up and tucked it into his jeans, carefully pulling himself together. If they were inside and getting together, the last thing he wanted to do was look like they had been on the cusp of doing the same thing.

Jackson would never let him live it down. On the other

hand, given how this day had gone and the fears he had been carrying about the two disappearing, he would prefer it to the alternative of them simply being missing.

In fact, when he did find them, Jackson would be getting a piece of his mind. His brother knew better than to just go MIA—he had to have known he was losing his cool about him.

As they made their way through the back door it occurred to him that it hadn't been locked. And it was odd that the blood had been around the back. Why, if the person punched in the glass of the side door, would they have walked around back?

The order of events was strange.

Had the person accidentally broken the glass and panicked? Had they not really been trying to go for the lock?

And why hadn't Jackson or Kelcie answered their phones or returned their texts? It wasn't as if the phones didn't work down here. He had just looked at his phone to call 911 and he'd had service.

Even if his brother was getting some action, he would have had a second to let him know he was okay. They had a system. Or at least Miles thought they did. And if they didn't, he was damned sure that Scarlett said she and her assistant did.

In the kitchen, there was an open beer sitting beside the sink. It was half empty, and the bent cap had been flipped haphazardly onto the floor. He moved to pick it up but changed his mind and left it lying where it had been carelessly tossed.

The door of the fridge was ajar, and he pressed it closed, surprised that the damned thing hadn't started beeping. Did that mean it hadn't been open that long? Or had it been left open so long that the beeping simply stopped?

The two lovers must have been in one heck of a hurry.

Yet, there had only been one opened beer.

"Jackson?" he called, walking toward the master bedroom. "You in here?"

There was no answer.

His heart pounded in his chest. He wasn't sure what exactly he feared the most.

"Kelcie?" Scarlett called from beside him. She slipped her hand in his.

Her hand was damp with sweat.

He found comfort in the fact that she must have been feeling as concerned as he was.

They moved down the hallway together, following the faint trail of blood. It was silent inside the main bedroom. The door was closed, and he rapped his knuckles on the wood, the sound echoing through the house.

He pushed open the door. The bed was in bloody disarray. Beside the side of the bed was the red shirt Kelcie had been wearing that morning. By the end of the bed was Jackson's blue plaid shirt.

Next to the door, and at the tip of Miles's sock, was a single brass shell casing.

Chapter Twelve

Deputy Trapper stood inside the cabin's living room tapping her pen against her chin as she took the report. She was wearing a pair of black UGG slippers and black-and-gray-plaid pajama pants, and her hair was pulled into a messy bun. She looked annoyed that she had been pulled from her bed at the main house to come out to the guesthouse.

"You know, bad news doesn't get better with time." She picked up her phone and typed away. "I let my husband know about what happened here tonight. As for my department, I want to keep a lid on this—at least from the public—as long as possible. That means we have to get this figured out in the next day or two."

Scarlett chewed at her lip, grateful her brother wasn't the one to show up at the cabin and out her, as she had expected. Now, it felt as if it was only a matter of time until the truth came out about who she truly was, and why she had come. Like her sister-in-law said, bad news didn't get better, yet she wasn't sure how she would deal with the fallout.

Her brother didn't even like her.

There was no proof that what had happened in the cabin tonight had anything to do with her, but the man Thomas had described sounded only too much like her former agent, and if he was slinking around, he would do anything to get at her.

For all anyone knew, maybe Kelcie hadn't even been there.

They had been in a hurry to get to the hospital when they had gotten off the trail. It was strange that they would have come back to the guest cabin before leaving. There were a number of things that just didn't make sense.

To top things off, if her brother found out that she had possibly brought trouble to his doorstep, any chance of their having a relationship was out the window.

If he kicked her off the ranch…she would have nowhere to run.

Maybe that was what needed to happen—maybe she needed to face Butch once and for all. If she was going to do that, she needed a gun. Or a man who was handy with the steel.

No.

She just had to wait for him to lose interest.

Not for the first time, she wished she could go to the courts and get a restraining order against him. She'd talked to an attorney about it, but the woman had told her the truth—restraining orders were only pieces of paper. And while the paper said he couldn't be near her or harass her, it did little for her when he followed her around the country and barraged her with social media garbage and spoofing phone calls. The man was a troll, and like most professional and smart criminals, he knew just enough about the limits of the law to keep from getting caught and charged with a crime.

Which was why it would have surprised her if he'd had anything to do with the bloody scene at their cabin. Since he'd been hunting her, he hadn't been so bold. He loved to hide behind his screens and occasionally pop his head up when she was standing in hotels or doing public events—he knew when she least wanted to be rattled and that was always when he struck. Yet, it was possible he'd been the one to hit the boy and his father.

If he was so angry, and if he had gotten the drop on her best friend and Jackson, why hadn't he just killed them here and waited for her to show up so he could finish her off once and for all?

It didn't add up.

Maybe this was all in her head and she was just aligning things that really didn't match up. There were plenty of older men that a five-year-old would describe as Santa. What other reference did they have?

She had never been a mother, she had no idea what a kid was capable of coming up with, but at that age, she doubted it was much more than that.

What was she thinking, being afraid of something and someone because of what a child had told her? Maybe this scene had nothing to do with the accident, maybe Kelcie and Jackson had gotten in a fight, maybe one of them had gotten hurt after they'd gotten locked out of the house while taking a dip in the hot tub.

From the state of the bedroom, they had started to take things there—or they had completed things there, she didn't want to know.

Maybe Mary was right, and they really had just gone the two hours south to the bigger hospital in Missoula, but if it was just for a sprained ankle or stitches…

"Ma'am, what did you say your name was?" Deputy Trapper asked, pulling her from her circular and nonsensical thoughts.

"Scarlett Leafletter. I'm just a guest here."

"Scarlett…" She nodded, but she frowned as she gave her an appraising once-over. "Pretty name. I know I've seen you somewhere."

She felt the heat rise in her cheeks, but she looked away in an attempt to hide the thoughts of this woman running across pictures of her as a child and possibly making the connection. It didn't seem likely, but she couldn't help herself from going to the worst possible outcome.

"Yeah, I've been working in film for a few years." She brushed back her hair and rearranged it into a new messy bun.

"I'm sure that's what it is." Emily smiled. "I'm sorry about your assistant. Like I said, I will be making some calls tonight, and I'll do everything in my power to find out what has taken place. For now, I recommend you guys move to the Chief Charlo cabin, Miles. If I need any further information or statements from you guys, I'll get ahold of you in the morning. You've put in a long one. Go get some rest."

She would have been slightly put out by the abruptness of the deputy's dismissal, but Emily was right, she was exhausted. It was probably evident on her face. Her eyes always tended to get dark bags underneath that the makeup artists commented on during shoots. She had always done her best to hide them with makeup, but no makeup was heavy enough to mask what had happened to them today.

It didn't take long for Miles to get Scarlett and her gear loaded up into the Mercedes-Benz and to make their way to the cabin just a few hundred yards down the road. It was slightly smaller than the other cabin, lacking an upstairs, but with the smaller size he actually felt more at ease.

After having cleared the cabin, and fearing making the same mistake twice, he escorted Scarlett inside.

She looked road worn, but still as beautiful as the first time he had laid eyes on her. He wanted to pull her into his arms and tell her how sorry he was about everything that had happened since she entered his life, but he found himself wondering if taking things to that level again was even more dangerous.

If he'd been paying more attention to details earlier, then maybe they could have had more of a chance of making a difference in his brother's disappearance. As it was now, all he knew was there was blood all over the damned place and even more questions than they had faced the rest of the day.

Nothing seemed to be going right.

To make matters worse, now his bosses knew about all his screwups and, without a single doubt, he'd be getting a phone call for a meeting in the near future. They'd be horrible business owners if they didn't just outright fire him for bringing chaos to their door.

Regardless of the circumstances, this day had gone all kinds of sideways, and he was the one standing at the epicenter.

Scarlett sat down on the leather Pendleton couch by the fireplace and let her hair out of her messy bun, letting it flow down and over her shoulders. She was so pretty, even when she wasn't trying.

He couldn't even begin to imagine how many men would give everything they had to stand in the same room as her, let alone kiss her as he had.

He still didn't understand why or how he had gotten so lucky—all he could come away with was that she was scared, lonely or tired. Heck, maybe it was just the search for vacation sex. People did it all the time—go to a place and meet someone who was no more than a ship passing them in the night. Or, in this case, a cowboy sharing the sheets for a romp around the arena.

He took a step toward the couch, thinking about how much he wanted to put his arm around her, but he didn't want to be there just for a good time. He didn't have a lot, but he had more to offer to someone than just his body.

Not that he wouldn't do it under different circumstances.

With so much on the line, and facing so much emotional turmoil, it seemed like taking her to bed tonight was wrong in every conceivable way…except when it came to the lust he felt. He wanted to rip her clothes off and make love to her right in the middle of the cabin's floor and in front of the fireplace—the day be damned.

When lust was leading the way, the only place a person was going to end up was at the corner of heartbroken and confused. For now, he'd take just getting some answers and keeping his job. All he had was being a cowboy—that was why she wanted him—and if he lost that there would be nothing left to him.

He made his way to the kitchen and made two ham and cheese sandwiches before opening a bottle of white wine. He poured them each a glass and made his way back out to the living room, but as he walked into the large room, he found her balled into the fetal position on the couch and fast asleep.

Her dark hair was splayed over the pillow in an angelic halo, and there was a loop of hair that had haphazardly fallen over her forehead. He desperately wanted to walk over to her and sweep the wayward hair from her skin but stopped himself. She was peaceful and perfect just the way she lay.

He was glad she had found a moment of respite, and it was far from him to want to steal a moment of this time from her. She needed a break.

The world around them was in flames, and for this brief moment in time, he could simply be here for her and be her greatest protector.

Chapter Thirteen

The morning came earlier than Scarlett would have liked. When she woke up, she had no idea where she was, but she was covered in a fuzzy blanket and found a down pillow under her head. Miles was sitting in the leather chair perched up awkwardly on his elbow, sleeping.

She watched him slumber, taking in the peacefulness of his features. His stubble had come in over the night, and she thought about how it would feel caressing against the skin of her face. Last night's kiss had been so special. And such a mistake.

It had been a moment of weakness to allow him that deep into her life. Yes, flirting was fun and tiptoeing along the line of impropriety was a thrill, but that was all she had wanted to do. To take it further was to risk making things immeasurably more complicated and would undoubtedly leave her feeling guilty the moment she left the ranch.

And that was what she had to do—leave.

As soon as she found Kelcie, they would have to search for another place. She'd been wrong in coming here and bringing her drama to the people she had once called family but were now nothing more than strangers.

She needed to concentrate on what needed to be done. And she wanted to talk to Thomas again. Maybe there was something they had missed, something he had seen that he had forgotten to tell her about.

Taking out her phone, she clicked it back on, and after a few moments, she was flooded with texts, emails and missed calls. Her voicemail was full.

She opened her messages, desperately hoping at least one of the dozens of messages was from Kelcie. Instead, most were from a barrage of different numbers, all from the same source: Butch.

Looking at the time stamps, the manic messaging had started around the time she had turned off her phone last night. As time wore on and the numbers changed, the messages grew shorter and angrier.

The first had read:

I hope I have your attention. If you would just talk to me, we could sort this out. You know you love me just as much as I love you.

Then it escalated into:

Answer me. If you don't, you'll never work again. I'll end you and your career.

And the most recent was simply skull emojis.

Among the messages were some in which he lost his temper, calling her every name in the book and telling her what she had done wrong as an actress and as a person. The following messages, a half hour later or so, would be messages of apology.

Emotionally, the man was all over the map.

Part of her actually felt bad for him. If she had only stayed in Montana, if she hadn't tried to break the mold, and if she had just played by the rules set forth by her father, she would have never found herself in this position or made this man spiral the drain.

Logically, though, and she'd heard it from Kelcie any number of times, stalking and a man's poor judgment was not her responsibility or fault. She was the victim.

Yet, she hated that word, *victim*.

It implied that she was powerless, that she was the damsel in distress who couldn't save herself.

She sighed. Then again, she ran here for a reason. She *was* the damsel, and she hadn't been able to free herself of this man's abusive grip. It sickened her that she was so weak.

She had even given in to him kissing her once, hoping that it would be so bad and lackluster that any desire he felt for her would be extinguished.

That had blown up in her face and became the day when everything had escalated.

She thought about the day she had first spent real time with him. She had been kind, talking about their families, and he had told her about his abusive, alcoholic father. His mother had put up with the abuse and fallen in line with his father's abusive behavior in hopes that if she just did what he asked things would get better. She didn't want to destroy their family, and she didn't want to take him and his brother away from their father.

In those days, he had told her, his mother feared the economic fallout of becoming a single mother. His abusive father had made it no secret that he would make life as hard as possible for her if she ever chose to leave him. She was a prisoner to her children, to her husband and to the circumstances of her life.

It was that story that had brought her closer to her own

personal demon. She had fallen for his sob story, one that had deeply paralleled her own.

Until recently, Scarlett hadn't truly understood why her mother had stayed with her father. Now, having endured the abuse that came with toxic relationships, she held an entirely new opinion. If she could go back in time, she'd have done anything to help her mother escape.

Miles stirred slightly in his chair, exhaling hard as though he was escaping some stressor in his dream. This simple action made a new wave of guilt flow over her. Even this man's dreams terrorized him. And she had a feeling it was because of her.

There was only one option.

She quietly got up from the couch and made her way to the back of the house, where she stood in front of the river and watched it pull against the banks. The world was always changing, just like the river, and no matter how hard she fought to escape the erosion that came with life, it would constantly tear away at her. If she was going to make a difference, she had to build her own walls. She couldn't wait for other people to save her.

She was strong. She could handle this. Perhaps, she could even stop any further harm from happening if she just took a stand.

Making sure the door was closed behind her, she made the call she was dreading the most.

He answered before it even rang.

"I had a feeling I would hear from you today. It's about freaking time. What else did I need to do to get your effing attention?" Butch asked, his voice sounding coarse and harsh, like he had spent all night talking in a smoke-filled bar.

She wouldn't have been surprised if she was right. It would help to make heads or tails of the text messages he had been sending throughout the night—he had gotten progressively drunker.

"Why is that, Butch?" she asked.

"If I've told you once, I've told you a million times. If you'd only listened, we wouldn't have any of these problems. But you refuse to take me seriously and you refuse to change. Why does it always have to be me who comes your way? Don't you care about me?"

She hated the way he rambled, spewing a myriad of thoughts and questions before she had a chance to even address one. He did it on purpose to control the conversations and to be able to tell her how stupid she was and how much she didn't listen.

"I'm listening now, Butch. What do you want?" she asked, trying to keep her thoughts under control when all she wanted to do was yell at him and tell him to leave her alone.

"I want you. I've wanted you from the first moment I laid eyes on you." He sounded beaten and battered by her, and it had a strange effect on her heart.

She hated him—how could he make her feel anything but just that?

She hated the way he made her feel.

She hated everything about him.

Yet, she owed him so much. She owed him for making her career. If she could just make him act right, they could have even continued working together and maybe she could have continued her upward trajectory in the business.

She turned to look inside, making sure that Miles was still asleep in the chair. His head was tilted back, and his eyes were closed. She turned back to the water, unable to think about him.

The cost would be too high if she kept playing Butch's game. Not only would it be her soul, but now it would also be anything she hoped to find—even if it was only a kiss—with Miles.

She wouldn't let this jerk stop her from living her life for another moment. And, if he had anything to do with what had occurred in the last twenty-four hours, she would seriously think about ways to end his.

"Butch, I don't want you. I've never wanted you. I've told you."

He laughed, the sound as dark as she knew his soul to be. "We both know that's not true. I felt it in the way you kissed me. I know you love me when I look into your eyes."

"Butch, you haven't seen me in three weeks. Not since New York. The last time you saw me, I can promise you what you saw in my eyes was as far from love as a human can possibly get."

"Why do you always have to play so hard to get with me? It drives me wild." The way he spoke the last word made her skin crawl.

Everything about this man made her want to take a shower.

"Where are you right now?" she asked, hoping he wouldn't play some stupid game like he always loved to do with her by either not answering or by trying to frighten her with his nearness.

"You know where I'm at."

So, it was one of those days where she was to let the games begin.

"I'm hoping that is Santa Barbara." She tried to sound cool, calm and collected, but her palms were beginning to sweat with nerves.

"Is that where you are?" he asked, sounding like the weasel he was.

"That wasn't the question. Just answer me. I want to know."

He laughed, the sound making her stomach ache. "See,

you do care about me. I knew it. You even want to know my whereabouts."

"Stop. Just tell me the truth."

"You want the truth?" The mirth in his voice was replaced with the sharp edge of rage. "I'm tired of your games."

Her games? She made a squeaking noise as she nearly choked trying to hold back her outburst.

"All you ever do is make me chase you," he continued. "It's getting tiresome, and I'm not chasing you anymore. If you want to get Kelcie and her little boy toy back, you're now going to have to come to me. If you want your friend back—I want you and five hundred thousand dollars. Cash."

The phone line went dead.

Chapter Fourteen

Miles had no idea how he'd actually slept. It had to have been pure exhaustion that had sent him into a near coma while he had been watching over Scarlett. When he woke up, however, he had absolutely failed at his job of being guardian.

Scarlett's blanket and pillow, the ones he had gently placed on her while she was sleeping last night, were neatly folded and stacked on the edge of the couch. She must have been up for hours, as he could smell the strong coffee permeating from the kitchen. As he stretched, he could hear her moving around in the other room and the sound of a metal utensil clanging against a bowl.

There was the sizzle of bacon, and the scent wafted out to him after a few minutes.

He stood up and stretched before checking his phone for messages.

Of course, there was one from Cameron and three from Emily, both wanting to meet up with him later today, but he sent Emily a quick text asking if they had gotten any new information on the whereabouts of his brother and Kelcie.

He waited, but the message remained unread, and so he checked his emails and then finally put away his phone and made his way to the kitchen. Everything could hold until he had more answers from the police.

With all the tech and eyes in the sky that law enforcement

had, he held out hope that he would at least have an idea if the ranch truck that Jackson had been driving was still in the area. If nothing else, it would be a place to start.

He made his way into the kitchen, where Scarlett was wearing a black apron with colorful peppers printed on the fabric over a pair of jeans and a white T-shirt. Her hair was pulled back into a long, beautiful ponytail that cascaded down her back, and for a minute his mind wandered to thoughts about pulling it while he was behind her in a moment of carnal pleasure.

He checked himself.

Last night he was as close as he wanted to come to carnal pleasure with her. He couldn't make that mistake again. Not with his job and his future riding on the line. However, that didn't mean he couldn't enjoy being around her while they tried to figure things out.

Even if he wanted to make her a part of his life, it wasn't like such a thing was even remotely possible. She was a traveler by nature. There was no way she would be happy just staying here on the ranch and settled down with a ranch hand. She could do so much better than him.

She had to have known it, too.

She turned around, but instead of greeting him with a smile, she looked upset. Her eyes were puffy and red, as if she had spent most of the morning crying. It made his entire core clench to see her like this.

"What's wrong?" he asked, not even bothering with false pleasantries.

"I… I don't even know what to say," she started, but she looked down at the spatula in her hand. There were bits of eggs on the plastic edge, and she turned back to where she had been working on the stove.

He didn't know if it was what had transpired between them

or the events of yesterday, and he wasn't sure he wanted to press too much out of the fear she would start crying. She was the most incredible woman, and if she started to cry, he would have to pull her into his arms. If he pulled her into his arms, he would have to kiss her. And if he kissed her, well... he wasn't sure he would be able to stop.

She couldn't cry. His heart couldn't bear it.

"Take your time," he said. He bridged the gap between them and moved to put his hand on her lower back but stopped himself at the last moment and instead gently took the spatula from her hand. "Here, you let me do this. You sit down."

She didn't fight him. Instead she simply nodded and moved out of his way. She grabbed two cups out of the cupboard and poured them each a cup of coffee, then sat down at the island in the center of the open kitchen.

He moved the eggs around the pan out of the need to move rather than any pressing cooking requirements as he waited in awkward silence for her to talk. Finally, after sipping on her coffee for what seemed like an hour, she ran her hand over her face and sighed. "There's no good way for me to talk about this," she started. "But I think I may know who has Kelcie and Jackson. He took them because of me, and he's holding them for ransom. I haven't told Emily yet, but we need to. Have you spoken to her?" All her thoughts bubbled over and spilled out into the room like boiling water.

He could already feel the burn.

He turned off the stove and grabbed the bacon out of the oven, taking a moment to get himself in order so he could be careful in his approach of this. He didn't want to come off like a jerk, but a part of him wanted to come at her about why she hadn't mentioned that it was possible she had played a role in their disappearances before now. Emily could have been working on that line all night. Instead, she told him *now*?

He tried to temper his anger. He didn't have all the facts. He couldn't make a judgment just yet, but if Scarlett had been lying to him and in doing so had put his brother in further danger…he couldn't forgive her.

"So, wait… You know the guy behind this *for sure*?"

She nodded, but she wouldn't meet his gaze.

He handed her a plate with eggs and bacon. Then he pulled a fork from the drawer and slid it over to her before getting his own. "Why would his taking them be your fault?"

She sighed, and there were tears welled in her eyes, but she took a deep breath. "His name is Butch Hafner. He is my former agent."

He was confused. "Why would your agent want to take anyone? Is he hard up for money or something? What am I missing?"

"He has been stalking me. I was trying to get away from him for a while, get a break from the chaos, and I came here. I think he must have found us, but I have no idea how. As for the money, he is just greedy. He knows how hard I've worked for it. It's just insult to injury. He wants to make sure I have nothing left."

The anger he was feeling shifted and became the fury that came with the prickling of fear. "How long has he been stalking you?"

"It's been unhealthy between us for a long time. I fired him six months ago as my agent, after he pinned me in a car and tried to assault me." She paused and cleared her throat as she struggled to keep her tears in check.

"You know…" He paused, seeing red. "Montana is one of those places where things go to disappear. We have a strong belief in taking care of our own problems. Especially when the problems are jackasses like him."

She smiled, but it didn't quite hit her eyes. "That's what I was hoping for when I came here. I just wanted him to stop, but now I want some vigilante justice."

"I can promise you, Scarlett, I'll let him buck."

Her eyes widened at his expression, and this time the smile worked up into her gaze. "If you do, you're not doing it alone. I'm not leaving your side."

It was strange how quickly she could turn him around. "That's good, because you better know I wasn't going to do this thing any other way." He took her hand and picked it up and gave it quick kiss to her knuckles. "I'm your cowboy vigilante."

She plucked a piece of egg off her plate, and she motioned for him to open his mouth. He took the bite, smiling as she fed him. "If you're going to go out there and take care of things, you're going to need your strength."

Her come-on caught him off guard, and he stopped chewing and stepped back. Looking away, he picked up his cup of coffee and took a long sip. She was out of his league. He couldn't fall into a situationship with this woman, no matter how badly every inch of him wanted to fall into her.

He sat his half-drank cup next to the sink and straightened his hair. His stubble had come in over the night, but there wasn't a thing he could do about it without running up to the bunkhouse. Maybe that wouldn't be a bad idea. It would give him a little time to gain perspective when it came to her; however, there was no leaving her side now.

If this stalker was bearing down on them, then he couldn't risk leaving her alone for even a moment. A desperate and angry man was more dangerous than a raging bull. At least with the bull, a person could see them coming.

He sent a quick text to Emily to let her know they needed to talk, but it didn't appear as though she had even read the last one he'd sent about checking on things. She must have been sleeping, having likely been working on the scene all night.

"Let's run over to the Saint Ignatius cabin and see if the cops still have it blocked off. If they do, maybe we can talk to the officer in charge of holding the scene. I can't seem to get ahold of Emily."

She looked slightly confused, but the expression was abruptly replaced with one of apathy. "Yeah."

He was glad she wasn't pressing for some deeper conversation about emotions or expectations. He didn't want to deal with anything like that right now. He didn't know what he wanted other than to keep his job and to find his brother… and he did want love, but that wasn't a risk he could even start to take.

She took a few bites of her breakfast. "Let me eat a little more, brush my teeth, and I'll meet you at the car."

He nodded. "Take as long as you need, babe." As soon as the moniker slipped from his lips the heat rushed to his face. He hadn't meant to call her that. He'd done so well in stopping the advance of flirtation between them and then he'd gone and done something stupid like that. Why couldn't his head and his heart get in line and get it together?

Her mouth turned into a cute little O shape, and then there was a sparkle in her eyes he couldn't have missed if he tried.

Not waiting for her to speak, or to complicate things, he turned on his heel and marched determinedly out of the kitchen and away from the woman who made him more confused than a bullfrog in a ballet class.

He grabbed the keys and pressed the fob to automatically start the vehicle and put the keys back down on the table by the door. He opened the door, expecting to see the early rays of the sun just starting to peek over the crests of the mountains on the other side of the valley. Instead, he was inundated by the red and blue lights and police vehicles that surrounded the white Mercedes-Benz.

"Excuse me? Can I help you?" he asked, calling to the cop that was standing directly in front of him.

The man turned and gave him a quick up and down scan, like he was looking to see if he was carrying any concealed weapons.

What in the hell was going on?

Why were they suddenly the ones being looked at like this?

Or, rather, why was *he*?

Just when he thought he was hopping from one confusing situation, he found himself landing in an even larger one. He would take the ballet class over this any day.

"Mr. Miller, do you know where we could find your friend Scarlett Leafletter?" the officer asked, his voice even and calm, not giving him any clues as to why he would be asking after Scarlett.

If they had found Kelcie and were here to deliver a death notice, he would have to be there to pick up the pieces. If the cops were there for that purpose, though, what about his brother? And he couldn't imagine they'd have their lights on if they were there for such a sensitive duty.

He had a few bucks lying around. If they arrested her, he was pretty sure he could afford to bail her out. Then again, why would they arrest her?

Did they think she had something to do with the disappearances?

She *had* been all alone on the ranch and puttering around outside the barn, according to her. That presumably could have given her plenty of time to make it down to the cabin and hurt or kill the two and make it back to the barn before he had arrived back with the Sullivan family.

As far as the police were concerned, he wouldn't tell them

a damned thing if it meant implicating her. He knew she didn't have anything to do with what was going on—she was the victim. She was the one being stalked and extorted.

By a man he'd never seen.

A man he hadn't even known existed until ten minutes ago.

Had she seen what the police were doing out here and then played him?

No. She wouldn't have done that to him. She wasn't some horrible creature.

He thought about the way her lips had felt against his. No monster could kiss him like she had or make him feel as he had felt when he had been holding her against his chest.

She was innocent.

"Sir?" the officer asked. The patch on his chest read Ramone.

"May I ask what this is in reference to?" he asked, trying not to sound unhelpful or like he was hiding anything—he didn't want him to get the wrong impression—he just wasn't about to leap blindly into the fire.

"Is this her rental car?" Ramone asked, not answering.

"It is."

"Did she spend the night here with you, Mr. Miles?"

He tried to keep his face placid and unreadable—the man didn't need to connect dots that hadn't and didn't need to be connected. "She did. And yes, she is inside. We were actually just on our way to the Saint Ignatius cabin to find Deputy Trapper."

The man's eyebrows shot up. "Oh? What did you need her for? Is there something you would like to tell me instead?"

He had a sinking feeling he was walking into a trap. "I just… I'd like to speak to her. Do you know where or when I can find her?"

"I'll let her know. For now, do you mind if we step inside?" The officer pointed toward the cabin.

The three other officers that were standing around the Mercedes-Benz were pretending not to be watching, as two of them tapped on their phones and the other was peering into the driver's side window with a flashlight.

"Sure, but what are you guys looking for in the car?" he asked.

"Let's go inside, and I'll tell you all about it."

He wasn't sure whether or not he should call an attorney, or at least his boss at the ranch, but if Emily was aware of what was going on he was sure she was at least letting her husband know. If they wanted him to have an attorney, they would find him one. That was, if they thought it was in the best interest of the ranch. As it was, he had the sinking sensation that his ass was hanging out in the wind.

Miles led him to the door and paused. If he let him go inside it was giving him a chance to snoop, but he had nothing to hide. He opened the door. "Let's sit down in the living room. I'll grab Scarlett and let her know you're here."

And see if she had known what had been going on outside before he'd awakened.

If she had…

The man nodded and strode past him, making his way inside. He walked into the living room and stood beside the couch, peering around the room until his gaze landed on Scarlett's suitcase, purse, and the coat she had been wearing yesterday morning when Miles had first seen her on the ranch.

"I'll be right back," Miles said.

"Take your time." The man walked over to Scarlett's bag and took a pen out of his chest pocket, using it to lift the straps of her purse and opening it slightly.

He rushed into the kitchen. "Scarlett?"

She was sitting at the island, picking at her breakfast, and she turned as he came storming inside. "What?" She looked at him and cocked her head and dropped her fork on the edge of her plate. "What happened?"

"Cops are surrounding your car and now there's one in the other room. Is there anything you haven't told me that I need to know? You have to tell me if I'm going to help." He moved close in hopes that anything they said couldn't be overheard from the other room.

"Why? Why would the police be looking into us?"

He shrugged and leaned over next to her on the counter. "Did you have anything to do with Kelcie and Jackson going missing? Anything at all?"

Her face fell, and she looked hurt. "Seriously?"

That wasn't exactly an answer, but if she didn't want to come out and just tell him, that was on her. From her expression, he felt like she was being earnest and hadn't done a thing wrong, but Scarlett was an actress. If she had done something, who was to say that she wouldn't have reacted the same way?

And yet even thinking this way about her, he felt like a jerk.

Why couldn't anything about this woman be simple?

"I hope you're telling me the truth." He pushed up and tilted his head toward the other room. "He's looking at your purse right now. I don't think we should leave him waiting."

She scowled as she stood up and swept past him as if he had upset her. Her reaction did nothing to assuage his uncertainty or make him feel like less of an ass. He ran both hands over his face as he sighed. Just when he thought about getting wrapped up with a woman, of course everything would hit the fan. He'd forgotten how complicated life had a way of becoming anytime feelings started to get involved.

He was amazingly attracted to her, and wanted her, but

if this was the chaos that she would bring to his life, he was going to have to take a moment to further reflect. If they did decide to ever take things to the bedroom, if he had the chance, he was going to have to gird his loins for a lifetime.

In the living room, the officer was seated next to her coat on the chair, and as he walked out the man smiled and slipped his pen back into his chest pocket. "Ms. Leafletter, Mr. Miller, I'm here to ask you both a few questions. This morning, we received an anonymous tip that there is a connection between you, Ms. Leafletter, and the disappearance of your assistant and a Jackson Miller. Do you know why we would have received such a tip?"

The color drained from Scarlett's face, and she shook her head. She drifted down to the couch like she was a feather. "I promise you, I didn't. I wouldn't. Kelcie's my best friend."

"Do you know who made the *anonymous* tip?" Miles countered. "I'm sure you have to have a clue if you think it was worth digging into."

The officer didn't acknowledge him. "Do you have any reason, Ms. Leafletter, that you and your best friend would be at odds with one another?"

She shook her head. "She and I get along really well. We have our rub points like any other friendship—we are together every day. We travel together. I'd never want to hurt her or see her put in danger."

The officer looked at him. "From the time you spent with these two women, would you say that she is telling the truth?"

Miles nodded. "Absolutely. They seemed to be very close and supportive of one another." So close, in fact, that he was the one who had felt like an outsider in their little club when he'd approached.

The officer stood up and took out his phone. "Had you

been in the cabin at any point before you arrived with Miles last night?"

She looked over at him with a scared expression. "No, I didn't even know how to get here, and I didn't have the code to get in if I had."

"Hmm," Officer Ramone said. "Do you know how your wallet would have gotten under the master bedroom's bed?" He pressed on the screen on his phone and pulled up a picture of a blood-covered beige Louis Vuitton clutch. "This is your wallet, isn't it?"

Tears welled in her eyes as she took the man's phone to look more closely at the photos, but he didn't know how she could have seen anything clearly with as bad as her hands were shaking.

"That's my clutch. I… I didn't even know it was missing." A tear streamed down her face, and as she struggled, Miles wanted to pull her away from the officer and tell her everything was going to be okay and that this was all just a big misunderstanding. "I wasn't in the cabin… I promise. And after they left to take Kelcie to the hospital, I swear I haven't seen either of them since. I swear."

Officer Ramone took the phone from her and put it back in his pocket. "I had a feeling you would say that." He turned to Miles. "Due to Emily Trapper's closeness to this case, we have removed her from the investigation. I will be your point of contact in this investigation."

Miles should have known. Emily had always been so good about answering whenever he had needed her about something on the ranch. He was only surprised that she hadn't told him the news about her being taken off the investigation herself.

"That's actually great news. We were hoping to talk to her about a potential lead," Miles said, trying to take some of the pressure off Scarlett. Her hands were in her lap, palms up, and she was staring vacantly into space. "Scarlett has been the victim of stalking. We think the man who was after her in California has found her here, and he may be the one behind the problems."

"Scarlett, do you have a picture of this man?" Officer Ramone asked.

"I don't." Scarlett shook her head. "There is probably one on his website, though I don't know how up-to-date it is."

"What is the man's name?"

"Butch Hafner. He is my former agent out of Santa Barbara. He has been calling me almost nonstop for the last six months. I changed my phone number. He follows me to events and threatens me."

"Have you reported this man and his behavior to the police in California?"

She looked at the office. "I was afraid that if I did, it would only make things worse. I was just hoping he would go away."

"Ma'am, do you have any evidence that he has been harassing you?" Officer Ramone asked.

She took out her phone and pulled up her call log. She handed it to the cop. "You can see how much he has called me. All the random numbers are spoofs by him. He knows I won't answer if he calls."

Officer Ramone stared at the phone. "Ma'am, you said you don't talk to him?"

She nodded.

"It looks as though you were talking to him this very morning. How do you explain that, if you are trying to avoid him? Wouldn't you have blocked his number?" He gave her a suspicious and cynical look.

"I forgot I talked to him!" Tears streaked down her face in rivulets, but Miles wasn't sure if they were out of stress, fear or frustration. "I called him because of everything that happened yesterday. I wanted to know if he was in Montana and if he had followed me. I was afraid he had something to do with Kelcie and Jackson. He told me that I was the only one who could get them back."

"Hold on," Officer Ramone said, holding up his finger. "Do you know if he is actually in the state?"

She opened and closed her mouth. "He didn't tell me."

The officer sighed. "Do you have a recording of this phone call? The one you *forgot* you made to a man who you said was stalking you?"

"It wasn't a long call, and I… I didn't record it. I just freaked out and needed to know. Thomas said the man who hit him looked kind of like Butch and…" Her words came out in a jumbled rush, but Officer Ramone stopped her with a wave of his finger.

"You can see where I'm having problems with your story, Ms. Leafletter? Most women, who have problems like that which you claim, call and report the activities out of fear. In California, I'm assuming its laws are similar to ours in Montana, but if you feel as though you are being intimidated by someone, it is enough to get a restraining order. I'm just struggling to understand why you didn't file for one if what you're telling me is true."

"I'm not lying. I swear. Look into him. If you can track or trace these numbers, you'll see it's him every time. You can have my phone, I don't care. Take it," she said, desperately trying to hand it over to the officer.

"Ms. Leafletter, as much as I want to believe what you are telling me, and about this man, you've given me no tangible evidence, no legal history of a crime, and if anything, the only clear evidence that you have supplied is of *you* contacting *him*."

She made a strange, strangled sound.

The officer put a reassuring hand on her shoulder. "We do take harassment and stalking very seriously. If you think you can provide evidence of him making you feel intimidated in any way, I recommend you going down to the crime victim advocate's office and having them help you file a motion for a temporary restraining order until you can stand in front of a judge."

"Thank you, Officer Ramone," Miles said, trying to protect Scarlett in any way he could. "Is there anything else we can do for you?"

"Ms. Leafletter, is there anything else you want to tell me, before I search your vehicle? Is there anything that you are hiding from me that I need to know?" Officer Ramone asked.

She shook her head.

"Okay." The officer dropped his hand from Scarlett's arm and gave Miles an appraising look. "I recommend that you both stay in West Glacier and don't leave the state in the next couple of days. I'm sure that we will be back with further questions about your brother and friend. As it stands, there's enough evidence on the scene to connect you, Ms. Leafletter, to their disappearances and possible murders. I won't arrest you today, however if we find anything further that implicates you, I'll be back with handcuffs."

Chapter Fifteen

Scarlett was beyond furious. Officer Ramone and his team of investigators were still outside, milling around her rental car. She could only assume they were waiting for a search warrant in order to gain entry to her vehicle.

The officer had been in such a big hurry to threaten her and tell her all the ways she had been delinquent in not adequately dealing with Butch that he'd not simply asked her if they could search. If he had, she wouldn't have stopped him, and yet she found a tiny glimmer of joy in the fact that they had to stand out there in the sun and wait.

They could sweat.

It was what he wanted her to do—unjustifiably.

Officer Ramone was wrong if he thought she had anything to hide. She looked out the front window of the cabin, her arms crossed over her chest as she tried to control her anger. She just couldn't believe the man could be so apathetic—it was like he had never been in a situation like hers and simply couldn't understand. That was probably exactly what it was. He just had no frame of personal reference. Or maybe he was used to dealing with false accusations or situations that were fueled by drugs and alcohol, and they had made him jaded.

As upset as she was, there was still a tendril of thought that the officer might have been justified in his assessment of her ability to prove malfeasance or criminal intent. She'd been stupid and lacking in judgment for not taking action against Butch and his threats and attempt to extort her sooner. It was just that she had been afraid of amplifying the problems. Maybe this all was in her head, though, and the calls were nothing more than election officials or something. Maybe they *were* just robocalls. Maybe she was making something out of nothing.

How had Butch driven her to the edge of madness?

No, she wasn't going to allow herself to be gaslighted by law enforcement or by her own self, and certainly not by Butch. Before she arrived, he had been harassing her and stalking her, and she wasn't just making it up. If she had the chance to talk to him again, she would make sure this time to record the conversation. She wouldn't make the same mistake twice.

Yet his threat had already been delivered. She had to go to him to get her friends back. And if the police didn't want to believe her, and they thought that she was falsifying her testimony or whatever, she would do it on her own.

The catch-22 was rage inducing. To nab this predator, she would once again have to allow him to be close to her, and in doing so, she would have to put her friends and herself at risk.

That was all on the condition that Butch was telling the truth and had kidnapped her friend. Knowing him, he really could have been anywhere in the world and was just playing mind games with her, anything to keep reminding her that he was the one in control and that no matter where she went, she was never outside of his reach.

She only wished she could make the officer understand and help.

Ugh. Well, he had helped *somewhat.* He'd told her she could go to the advocates. But without any tangible proof of

Butch's harassment and stalking, the word of a little boy who said he thinks he saw Santa wasn't going to cut it.

She really was on her own.

"Are you okay?" Miles asked, walking up from behind her and putting his hand on her lower back.

The simple action made her jump, and she threw back her hand, hitting Miles and making him jolt. "Sorry," she said, trying to calm herself after his jump scare.

"You're okay. We're going through a lot right now. You've every right to be jumpy. However," he said, lifting a mug of freshly made coffee that was now dripping down his arm, "I'm going to have to dry myself off." He lifted the mug for her to take.

She took the cup. "You're not burnt, are you? Oh, my goodness, I didn't hear you coming."

"Don't worry," he said, giving her a kind smile. "If anything, I'm impressed with your martial art skills. Nobody is going to get the drop on you."

Her thoughts went instantly to Butch and his stupid round face with his white beard and his graying hair. How many times had he gotten the drop on her at events, only to stand in corners and leer at her until he could try and get her alone?

Her hands started to shake, and the coffee sloshed against the cup.

Miles reached up and cupped her hands and the mug with his own. "Maybe caffeine wasn't such a good idea."

"That's not it." She couldn't meet his gaze, and instead she tilted her head back and let out a long, calming exhale. She didn't have to be scared right now. There was no boogeyman here to get her, it was only her thoughts. "I'm fine. Really."

"You can try and tell whomever you want that, but I'm not an idiot." He took the cup from her hands and sat it down on the stone-covered table by the front window. "Why didn't you tell me about the phone call?"

Her stomach dropped. "I thought I did. I told you I knew he had Kelcie and Jackson—that was because of the call."

He was watching her in a way that made her feel like she was being questioned by Officer Ramone once again, and she hated it.

"Or, at least I'm pretty sure Butch took them." She ran her hand over her face. It smelled of coffee. "I mean, it's possible he was just playing me when I talked to him. Maybe he could tell I was upset or something, but he told me right before the line went dead, 'If you want to get Kelcie and her little boy toy back, you're now going to have to come to me.'" She tried to mimic Butch's weak, mid-register voice. "He told me I would have to pay him five hundred thousand dollars. Which is almost the exact amount I have saved in my liquid accounts. It's like he knows. It was so weird that I'll never forget it."

"Why would he ask for money? Is he struggling financially?"

"No," she said, shaking her head. "He is a trust-fund kid. He can go anywhere in the world at any time. His father created the artificial heart valve and sits on the board for the AMA. He's fine."

"So, explain the ransom."

"He… When…" She paused, picking at her fingernail. "When I left home, I walked away with nothing. He told me that every penny I ever made was because of him. Apparently, he wants it all back."

"I'm so sorry." He took her hand in his and turned away to look out the window at the police. "Are they going to find anything in the car that we are going to need to worry about or explain?"

"No. I promise. And I promise, I'm telling you the truth

about Butch…and about everything. I wouldn't lie to you." She hated how desperate she felt to be believed and validated by him, but she needed him in her corner so badly.

"I believe you, I do." He kissed the back of her hand and nodded.

They watched as Officer Ramone came sauntering back up the path and to the front door. They waited for him to knock before Miles let go of her hand and went to answer. He opened it up, and the officer had a dour expression on his face. "How's it going out there?"

Officer Ramone looked from him over to Scarlett, and the way he studied her made her want to shrivel up into a tiny ball on the floor. "We have yet to receive our search warrant from Judge Donovan. However, while I was waiting for his response, I pulled up a little bit of information about you, Ms. Leafletter."

Her blood drained from her face and down out of her chest, and she glanced to the floor to see if it had really, truly leached from her body.

"Does your friend here know your true identity? Does anyone?" Officer Ramone sent Miles a quizzical glance.

Miles looked shaken, and he stepped back from her as if she had just struck him.

"I'm sorry, Miles. It's not a big deal…" she started, but even as she spoke, she knew how damaging the next revelation would be to the man who she had, just moments before, promised complete honesty. Her promise hadn't even lasted five minutes.

"What isn't? *Who are you?*" Miles spat the words like they were bile on his tongue.

She wanted to tell him that she was the woman he had met, the woman who was devoted to her friend and would stop at nothing to make sure she was safe. And she wanted to tell him that she was everything he was looking for, but all she could think about was who she really was—flaws and all.

"I'm Teri Trapper. I'm Cameron's sister. He doesn't know I'm here, and he doesn't know my pseudonym. I came here to hide from Butch. Everything else I've told you about myself is true. I swear."

"You mean just like you swore you were telling me the truth before?" Miles's anger rippled through his voice. He turned and walked to the door but looked back over his shoulder at her as he opened it. "You know, from the moment I met you I felt something. I thought it was..." He paused, making her wonder what he was going to say, but instead his scowl deepened and his eyes darkened. "I just didn't know what I was really feeling should have been suspicion."

He strode out the door and slammed it behind himself.

Whatever they had going on, it was irrevocably and unquestionably over.

Chapter Sixteen

The police wouldn't let Miles anywhere near Scarlett's car. Or wait, was it Teri's?

Given how many times she had lied to him in just their short amount of time together, he had a feeling that if he stuck around, the police would next tell him that there were a hundred kilos of cocaine in her trunk, and she was a drug runner from Mexico.

Nothing about this lying woman would surprise him anymore.

He was glad he hadn't taken things further last night. For once, he had dodged a bullet.

One of the officers, Deputy Burns, sidled over to him, his right thumb stuffed under the top of his utility belt. "How's it going?"

He wasn't sure what to make of the man's informal greeting, especially considering how it had been going with Ramone. "I've had better days. You guys find anything?"

The man shrugged. "This your girlfriend's rig, sir?"

"No, she is just a guest who's staying at the ranch. And I'm Miles Miller. I'm only a guide hired to keep her...*entertained*." After last night's kiss and the revelations this morning, it felt strange devaluing Scarlett to the level of another visitor on the ranch. She was so much more and had brought so much drama into his life that she had quickly embedded herself into the frontrunner position in his life. Who was keeping whom on their toes was up for debate.

Burns sighed. "I completely understand. Lots of dudes have been coming up here lately to play cowboy and cowgirl. You must get some doozies."

He hadn't had that many paying guests at the West Glacier Ranch, but when he'd worked as a hand at the Joy Luck Ranch in Somers, he had seen more than his fair share of poor behavior and rudeness. That being said, at least half of the people he'd worked with were kind and generous, many even becoming friends who had returned to the Joy Luck year after year just to see him again.

His least favorite guest of all time had been a moderately wealthy civil engineer with family money who had gotten upset when Miles had not been at their beck and call during the night to light their path while they'd been on an overnight horseback ride up into the Swan Range. He had been up all night with the flu and hadn't been able to get out of his sleeping bag, let alone hold a flashlight for someone else to pee.

The man had even gone so far as to call after he got back and complain about the lack of safety concerns and how lazy Miles had been on the trip.

It had been that complaint that had nearly gotten him fired. His former boss, Drake Rex, hadn't believed him about the stomach flu and paid him his weekly wages and ordered him off the ranch. Chloe had gone to Drake to talk. He'd gotten his job back, and that was the gateway to Chloe and Drake's relationship—and the real end of theirs.

After all he had done for the place and the guests he'd brought in and made happy, Miles had been incredibly hurt. Sick was sick whether a person was on the mountain or in the comfort of their own bed. He couldn't pick the time, and he certainly hadn't been in a position to do anything more than he had. It hadn't been his fault he had gotten sick on the trail.

Come to think about it, Drake Rex may have been the biggest source of problems in his professional life. He always had something or someone he was complaining about. And no matter how hard his employees worked, it seemed as though it was never quite enough. In one weekend, Miles had brought in forty thousand dollars in revenue thanks to a repeat client. Instead of congratulating him and thanking him for his great work in keeping clients and guests happy, Drake informed him that he would need to do it again.

His indifference was one of the reasons Miles had been only too happy to take his last check and leave. It also hadn't hurt that he was leaving his ex-girlfriend on the ranch to take over his place as head guide. Miles kind of found a wicked sense of joy in the idea of her having to fill his shoes and play nice when it was often nothing more than a thankless job.

"Miles, is your brother Jackson Miller?" Burns asked, pulling him from his thoughts.

Miles nodded. "Yeah, did you hear from him?"

The officer shook his head. "Actually, I was wondering about where your brother was staying. Did he live out here on the ranch with you or did he have another place he's been renting? The information we have on him in our system has him still living at your parents' home. However, when we went to check his residence, no one there had heard of him, and it appeared as though that house changed hands."

Miles sighed. "Yeah, my parents passed away shortly after a car accident a few years ago. My siblings and I had to sell it to take care of their medical bills and care. Jackson had been staying at my old apartment—he took over my lease. If you want, I have keys and I'd be happy to take you over there."

He doubted they would find anything about his brother,

at least nothing that he hadn't already known—that Jackson could be a bit of a slob, he didn't own a vacuum, and he liked to drink Miller Lite. He had no doubt that the garbage can at the end of the kitchen counter was probably spilling over with empty cans.

Burns cast a glance over at the other officer standing by the car. "I'm going to take a run over to Jackson's apartment, see if we can dig anything up there about his possible whereabouts. If you guys need me, just call. Shouldn't be too long."

The other officer sent them a finger wave in acknowledgment.

"We can jump in my car," Officer Burns said, pointing in the direction of the squad car parked in the back of the line of three. It was a compact sedan, and it was still running, as though he assumed he would be leaving at any moment.

"We?" Miles asked, surprised that the officer would want him along for anything.

"Yeah, I'm going to need your key and your permission to enter the premises—that is, if your name is still on the rental agreement."

He was angry and hurt at Scarlett's lies, but at the same time, he didn't want to leave her on the ranch alone. She needed someone in her corner. However, she had Officer Ramone. But Miles had promised her he wouldn't leave her alone.

That had been before she had promised him she was telling him the truth.

His anger started to seep up from the edges of his being once again.

"Let's go." He turned and gave the cabin one last look before walking over to the man's patrol car and stepping inside.

The ache in his gut grew larger as Burns stepped inside and they drove off.

He watched the ranch disappear in the side mirror as they made their way to the highway and toward his old apartment. He regretted leaving her, but he couldn't help but wonder if he hadn't gone, if he would have regretted staying.

SCARLETT STARED OUT the front window, watching as Miles got into the cop car and drove away. "Where are they taking him?" she asked Officer Ramone.

He tapped his finger on his belt as he leaned forward and peered out the window to see what she was talking about. "I couldn't tell you."

She wasn't sure which way he meant the words, but she knew regardless of inflection, the answer she would receive from the tight-lipped officer would be the same. "Are they going to bring him back?"

A new fear twisted through her—that of being truly alone.

He'd promised her he would stay, but she had screwed everything up. If only none of this had happened.

Yet, what else had she expected? She had come here knowing about Butch and his problems, then she had kept her truth from the one man who had wanted to help her. She could hardly blame him for getting in the cop car and driving away.

She wished she could go back in time and redo everything.

She wouldn't have come here.

She wouldn't have put Kelcie and Jackson in harm's way.

Hell, if she could have gone back in time, she wasn't sure she would have ever left this ranch in the first place. Nothing had gone right in her life since she had thought she had escaped.

She closed her eyes and sighed as she considered what a naive child she had been when she went running off to Hollywood. Her story was like thousands of other women's—coerced and used, then disregarded and minimized and made to feel so small that they quit on their dreams, or worse, were killed.

She couldn't let Butch win. If he did, and she gave up on her dreams and on the woman she wanted to be, then she might as well just hand over her soul. She'd always think about what would have been if she'd fought the man harder.

Yet, how was she going to fight a shadow? Especially if she was nothing more than his puppet.

"You know, you can just look through my car. I don't care and I have nothing to hide."

At least, nothing *anymore.*

Officer Ramone looked at her with surprise. "Are you sure? It is within your legal rights to wait until we have obtained our search warrant. And so you know, you are welcome to retain an attorney at any time."

"Am I under arrest?" she asked.

"Not yet, but you not disclosing your true identity to me has done nothing for your credibility. And, from the look on your boyfriend's face, I'm going to say it did nothing for your budding relationship, either."

She huffed but tried to cover the sound with a cough. "There's no relationship. We are just friends."

"You do know that I've been in control of many investigations in my time as a law enforcement officer. I've made a living out of telling when people are lying to me. And trust me when I say I have had a lot of people lie to me, and most are far better at it than you—actress, or not."

She didn't know how to respond. Instead, she grabbed the fob off the table by the door and handed it over to the officer. "Here. Have at it."

He took the keys and gave her an appreciative dip of the chin. "Why don't you go ahead and walk out here with me?"

He opened the door and waited for her to step outside before closing it behind them.

She followed in his footsteps as he walked toward the Mercedes-Benz.

"Do you mind if I look in the trunk?"

"Go right ahead." She waved in the direction of the car.

He hit the button on the fob and the trunk latch popped open and the lid started to rise. Inside the trunk, lying on a bloodied white mink blanket were two pairs of steel handcuffs. Each pair was slathered in sticky, drying blood.

She fell to her knees. "Oh, my God."

Her breath caught in her throat, and she slumped forward as hot rivulets of tears streamed down her face. A faint wind kicked up, carrying the scent of iron-rich blood in her direction, and it made her stomach turn sour.

Officer Ramone stepped closer to her and unclicked the metal cuffs from a leather case on his belt. "Scarlett Leafletter, would you please lay down and put your hands behind your back? I'm placing you under arrest."

Chapter Seventeen

After banging on the cheap wooden front door of his old apartment, Miles unlocked it, and the yeasty smell of a stagnant hot room wafted toward him and Officer Burns as he opened the place up. The studio apartment in the basement of the landlord's house was as he expected it—filled to the brim with empty beer cans and there were heaps of clothing in piles around the main room.

It would have never looked like this when he lived there, but aside from the clutter, thankfully his brother didn't seem to have let it get too deeply into disrepair to threaten his sublet agreement.

"You can do whatever you need. I gotta say, though, it doesn't look like he has been around."

Burns stepped around him and made his way into the apartment. "Where is the mailbox for this place?"

Miles pointed out toward the road. "It's the black box by the road."

The officer nodded. "I'm going to request to get a warrant to locate your brother's last cell phone ping, but that can take some time when we are working through cell phone companies."

"I appreciate that," he said. "My brother and I are pretty close. He has always been a good apple, and I just can't see why anyone would want to hurt him."

Burns walked toward the kitchen table that sat in the middle of the open kitchen. He stared at the stack of papers that were sitting on the surface. He had his thumbs stuffed under his Kevlar vest as though he was trying to intentionally keep from touching anything.

"Did either of you know Kelcie or Scarlett before they came to the ranch?"

"No." He thought about Scarlett and who she really was. "Scarlett said she had looked into the ranch before she came. Based on who she really is and what she said, you should really ask if she knew me before she arrived, not the other way around."

Burns looked up from the stack of papers. "Interesting. It sounds like you don't care for her very much, that you don't think she is worthy of your trust. Is that true?"

When the man put it like that it had a way of stinging.

He wasn't sure what he truly thought or felt when it came to Scarlett, but there was one thing he knew—she was more than met the eye. As for malicious intent and guilt, he wasn't sure.

"I think that she's really afraid."

"Do you think that she could have had anything to do with her friend's disappearance? Was there any sort of friction between the two that you noticed?" the officer asked.

"Far from it. They seemed like they were really close, and I can't say that I got any impression that there were issues between them. They seemed like sisters." Miles closed the door to the apartment behind him.

Officer Burns moved out of the kitchen toward the small bathroom and peered inside. "Hmm."

Officer Burns made Miles deeply uncomfortable, but he wasn't sure if it was because of the situation or if it was because they were standing in his former apartment, the one he had shared with his ex-girlfriend Chloe from the Joy Luck

Ranch. Jackson had taken over the lease, but he hadn't spent much time in this place. In fact, he had intentionally avoided it thanks to the memories cast by the location.

Burns walked down the hallway to the single bedroom and opened the door. He motioned for Miles to come over. Inside the room was a dresser with open drawers and socks and underwear scattered over the edges. The closet was open, and empty hangers littered the floor. The bed was pristine, with blue sheets and a matching quilt. Each of the pillows was placed carefully at the head of the bed. It ran in strange juxtaposition to the chaos of the bedroom.

"Is this how your brother always lives?" Officer Burns asked.

"My brother can be a bit of a slob, but did you see his bed? It's made."

"I noticed the same thing. Did your brother have a duffel bag or suitcase that you know about?"

"Do you think that my brother planned to abduct Kelcie or something?" Miles tried not to sound affronted. However, the idea sounded so out of left field to him that he wasn't quite sure what to make of it. "That doesn't make any sense."

The officer walked over to the closet and peered inside. "There don't appear to be any clothes in here, or a suitcase." He turned back to face Miles. "And as for people making sense, that's like thinking you can assume what people will do. People never cease to surprise me."

He appreciated that the man didn't seem to be putting him on trial, but it was so strange standing in the bedroom talking to a police officer, the same bedroom where he had spent many nights with Chloe.

He hated thinking about her and how she had cheated on him, possibly exactly where they were currently standing. "I have found that it's the people we think we can trust the most that always disappoint. And often, it's the people that we least expect who come through in the end."

"It sounds like you've been through the wringer."

"I'm sure you've had your fair share of relationships, too."

The officer huffed. "I don't know that I'd call them relationships or opportunities to watch train wrecks up close and personal." He gave his slight laugh. "I'll leave it with cops don't have a reputation for failed relationships for no reason."

"I think that's one thing that we cowboys have in common with you." He laughed. "Is there anything else you were hoping to find here? Do we still need to keep looking, or are you ready to head back to the ranch?"

"I know you don't think that your brother had anything to do with Kelcie's disappearance, but I have to say I think it's odd that his clothing and personal items have been rifled through, and his suitcase is missing. Even his toothbrush was gone from the bathroom. It looks like he was planning an extended stay somewhere, or with someone. He didn't have a girlfriend that you know of, did he?"

"No. My brother was kind of a lone wolf type. I think he likes several women right now and isn't ready to be tied down to one of them."

"I envy him that. He needs to get it all out of his system. It makes life a lot easier when you get a little older. For me, I think I've figured out what I want in life. Or at least I thought I had, right up until my current divorce."

"I'm sorry to hear about it. Those can be tough."

"Did you ever go through one?" Burns asked.

He shook his head. "I was just living with a woman, and she managed to break my heart by cheating on me with my boss from my former job. Now she has my job and she's working arm in arm, or hopping into bed, with my former supervisor. It's one of the reasons I had to go to work for the West Glacier Ranch."

"You're lucky you found out who she was before you made a real mistake."

He wanted to argue that falling in love with her had been the real mistake, but he didn't push the issue with the man who was clearly jaded.

"Do you know the names of the women your brother was dating? Or, if any of them are the jealous type?" Officer Burns asked.

"No. My brother and I don't really have that kind of friendship. Even if we did, he is the kind who keeps things close to his chest."

Burns smiled. "You gotta love brothers." He looked back at the table one more time as he stopped at the front door. His cell phone vibrated and started to play Five Finger Death Punch. He pulled it from his pocket and put up his hand, motioning for Miles to stay put as he stepped outside.

Miles could hear him speaking. There was something about an arrest. He promised whomever he was on the phone with that he'd be there in twenty. If nothing else, at least they were done poking through his brother's apartment. It felt awkward and wrong, and he could honestly say he never wanted to step foot back in the place.

He walked over to the table and took a peek at the papers Burns had been so interested in. The paper on the top was a credit card bill. He moved the envelope covering the amount due. He had to read the number twice. A lump grew in his stomach. His brother owed more than thirty thousand dollars, and the compounding interest was swamping him.

Why hadn't Jackson told him? He would have helped him out.

That number was more than half of what his brother made

annually. No wonder he had been so desperately interested in coming to work for him at the ranch.

As soon as he found him, they would need to talk. That was *if* he found Jackson and his brother was still alive.

His brother had made some mistakes in life, and he liked to party and gamble, but Miles hadn't thought getting himself in this deep of water was one of them. It made him wonder what other kinds of issues his brother was having.

His mind whirled with possibilities. If his brother was that far in debt, he had to have been desperate to get out. If he was desperate enough, would he have or *could* he have kidnapped Kelcie? Perhaps he was just biding his time until he made his demands known.

Scarlett wasn't poor, and as it so happened, she didn't come from a poor family. She would have been a perfect mark to use for a huge payout in a kidnapping. Miles wasn't a criminal, but if he wanted to get Scarlett to do what he wanted, he could have gone after her best friend.

While Jackson had his faults, he'd never been arrested for a crime, and he'd never had run-ins with law enforcement. In high school, he had done well but had liked to skip class any chance he got to spend the days hiking around the mountain, and hunting or fishing. He was just a good ole Montana boy.

His parents would have rolled over in their graves if they knew what he was wondering about his brother. They had raised them to have integrity and honor, but they had also taught them not to live outside their means.

Jackson wasn't a suspect in Kelcie's disappearance. No. Scarlett had already told him that her stalker had basically admitted to taking them. They just needed to dig deeper into the creep.

Officer Burns opened the door and waved for him to come

outside as he hung up his phone. There was a strange expression on his face. “We need to hit the road. Let’s go.”

He followed the officer up the stairs and out to his squad car. As he got in and buckled up, Burns opened his computer that was mounted between them and started to type.

“I don’t know if you heard,” Officer Burns started, not even bothering to look up from his computer, “but your client, Ms. Leafletter, was arrested. She is on the way to jail, where she will await arraignment.”

He jerked. “What? What was she arrested for?”

“Officer Ramone believes there is enough information to charge her with murder.” Officer Burns shrugged. “I have no idea what went on after we left the ranch, but if you’re her friend, you should make some calls to lawyers. She is going to be facing some major obstacles.”

“She didn’t *kill* anyone.” He balled his hands into tight fists, readying himself for a fight to protect the woman he had come to secretly love.

Chapter Eighteen

She felt absolutely sick. In her entire life, Scarlett had never imagined that she would find herself waiting in the jail near the Flathead County Courthouse after being cuffed, stuffed, booked and waiting for arraignment. If they offered bail, she would need to make a call. To whom, she wasn't sure. Kelcie would have been her go-to, but now…

There were five other women in the jail cell with her. One was lying on the only concrete slab and was asleep or doing a great job of pretending. A blonde sat in the far corner, her knees tucked into her chest, and she was mumbling incoherently. Two were sitting together and whispering, and the last stood at the front of the cell, holding the bars and watching whatever was going on outside their unit.

In her wildest nightmares, she couldn't have come up with a situation like this.

She wanted to cry, to scream to the universe that she was being unjustly treated, but given how the world had been bearing down on her since she'd gotten here, to speak out would only lead to more problems.

When she stood in front of the judge, she would plead not guilty, but she would need a good attorney. Hopefully, the judge would see things from her perspective and have leniency. She had been framed for a crime she had most definitely not committed, and just because there was evidence of something heinous, Officer Ramone had made a mistake.

The brunette woman who was standing at the front of the cell turned. "Someone is comin'. Who ya'll think they gonna see next?"

Scarlett stood up from her place against the wall and smoothed the jeans she had bought online from the ranch supply store before she'd come to Montana. No matter how much she dressed the part, she would never be able to fit into this rough place where justice was an illusion. Apparently, she wasn't the only one faking an appearance.

The jailer walked up to the bars. "Ms. Falconer, you need to step back from the bars," he ordered the brunette.

The woman let go of the steel bars and stepped back with a tip of the head.

"Ms. Leafletter, would you please approach the cell door?"

Her stomach lurched and cold sweat broke out on the base of her neck at the sound of her name being called. The judge must have been working fast.

Her feet felt as though they were encased in concrete as she made her way to the door.

"Turn around and put your hands behind your back," the man ordered.

She did as she was told, but her hands were trembling. He slapped the cold steel handcuffs around her wrists. They seemed heavier than the ones Officer Ramone had put on her at the ranch, but it could have just been in her head.

The jailer led her out of the holding area and to the stairwell. "Officer Ramone wants to see you in his office."

"Do you know why?"

He shook his head. They didn't share another word until she was standing outside Officer Ramone's office and the man tapped on the heavy oak door. "I have Ms. Leafletter here to see you."

"Come on in."

The man opened the door and waved her inside. He gave her a scowl as she passed by, and the look made her feel as though she was the biggest criminal on earth, and he was the one passing judgment.

So much for being innocent until proven guilty.

"Thank you, Taylor. You can go," Ramone said.

The man tipped his head and closed the door as he made his way out.

"Did you change your mind about me? Decide that I'm not actually one who would go around murdering my friends?" she asked, suddenly angry. She didn't know what hit her, if it was her anxiety or the nerve of him having put her in this position, but she couldn't help the sensation of rage that was bubbling up from her core.

"Actually, I did want to talk to you a little bit. Why don't you take a seat, and then I will take off those cuffs?"

She frowned. This man had been a pain in her ass since the moment she had met him and now he was offering to chat and make her comfortable. She couldn't trust him. However, she sat down as he asked and turned so he could unlock the cuffs behind her back.

"Have you heard how Thomas and his father are doing?" she asked.

He stood up and walked over. "Thomas is still in the hospital. They're trying to get in touch with a family member who can take him. It sounds like he doesn't have any other family. I don't know how that is going to work out. As for Aiden, he's still in critical condition. They have placed him in a medically induced coma."

Thomas had been so scared, and she could only imagine

what he was feeling now that his father was standing at the brink of death.

She could hear the metal key move into the lock and the snap as he opened the cuffs and removed them from her wrists. "There, that has to feel better. Doesn't it?"

"Much." She turned to face his desk and rubbed at the place on her wrist where the steel had chafed her skin. There was a set of marks where the cuffs had started to cut in because the jailer had pressed them too tight.

"So," Ramone said, walking around his desk as he dropped the open cuffs onto it like some sick reminder of the damage he could inflict. "I have been looking into your former agent, Butch Hafner. How well do you know this man?"

A sense of relief flooded her. This was the last thing she had expected from the man who had arrested her. "He was my film agent for two years. We spent some time together when I was filming. He liked to drop in and take me out to lunch and things. He always called me his 'Big Fish.'"

"I bet that felt pretty amazing, being an up-and-coming actress who was being fawned over by her agent, didn't it?"

She didn't like his tone, but she tried to ignore it. "Yes. It's always nice to be appreciated."

Something she doubted he felt very often.

"Uh-huh. Did he ever tell you much about his background?"

She thought back for a moment. So much of what he had said to her had been in one ear and out the other, as she had taken it mostly for small talk—at least, at first. "I remember him saying he was from the New England area originally, and his father was abusive. Oh, and he graduated from Harvard. Beyond that, I'd really have to think. Why?"

"I've been doing some digging."

"You mean like you did on me?" she spouted, more than

aware that her best bet would have been to be quiet, but she simply couldn't help herself.

"You're the one with bloody cuffs in your trunk. Do you really think you should be talking to me that way? I would be more than happy to drop you back in your jail cell."

She sighed. "I know. Sorry. I can't help it..." She ran her hand over the back of her neck. "Just tell me one thing."

"What?"

"Do you really think I had something to do with my best friend's blood getting in my trunk?"

"Well, for starters, we don't know whose blood that was, or if those cuffs were on your friend and Jackson at any time. Until the tests come back, County Attorney Yates doesn't actually think we have enough to formally charge you."

"Wait... So you're letting me go?" She couldn't hold back the relief and excitement in her voice.

"Officially, I can hold you up to forty-eight hours to question you in your possible role in this crime. If you don't want to go back down to the cell for the remaining forty or so, I would appreciate it if you could drop the attitude and work with me in getting as much information together as possible to help your friend—who is hopefully still alive. Capisce?"

"Fire away. You know all my secrets now. I've got nothing else to hide." She opened her hands like she was opening a book.

"Great. Now, did you know that Butch Hafner was also known by another name?"

"No. I'm surprised that he never mentioned it to me, but it's not uncommon for people in our line of work to assume pseudonyms for privacy and safety."

"I can understand the desire, especially nowadays. However, this guy's legal name is now Butch Hafner. Before he was known as Butch Harrington."

"Why would he change his name?"

Ramone smiled. "That's what really made me start digging into him. I had the same question. I went down the rabbit hole, and it appears as though this guy was a felon."

A cold chill ran down her spine. "And as for Harvard, there is no record of him ever attending or graduating from the Ivy League school. However, he did grow up in Boston and he lived near the college, but in a different part of the city."

"Everything I thought I knew about this man was a lie." Her voice was flat at the realization of how much she had been lied to and manipulated by Butch.

She hated him.

Actually, hate wasn't even the tip of the iceberg of loathing she felt at the mere thought of him. She had never wanted to kill someone, but for a brief moment she could understand how a person could be pushed to the extreme.

"You would be surprised by how often I hear people say that."

She wasn't surprised. There were sheep and wolves in the world, and she knew both kinds. If only she hadn't been the one to show her woolly throat to the predator.

"What felony was he convicted of?" she asked, a thick numbness settled over all the feelings that had been sifting through her until all she could feel was the cold steel arms of the chair pressed against the bottom of her forearms.

She pressed her fingers into the edge of the chair until her knuckles cracked and she could feel the bones under the pads of her fingers press against the metal until it hurt.

"He got himself wrapped up in an undercover sting. Apparently, he was involved in human trafficking and the abuse of underage girls."

She stared at Ramone. His eyes were dark brown and there

were heavy, fatty bags under his eyes. His left eye twitched slightly as they looked at one another.

"He was convicted four years ago. Two years later, he legally changed his name and filed to have his record expunged."

"Was it?"

"If it had been, I wouldn't be reading about it in our database."

At least the court system and one judge had seen him for who and what Butch really was—a criminal.

"Do you finally believe me about him being a stalker?"

Ramone tapped his fingers on the desk. "I think that a zebra can't change his stripes. That being said, I think that if you want to handle this and him correctly, we need to get some evidence that we present to a judge."

She reached over to Ramone and took his hand in an awkward grip. "Thank you, Officer Ramone. Thank you for finally understanding."

"Is there anything else you can tell me about Butch—if you do think he was the one responsible for these disappearances—that could help us pin him down? Do you know where he is?"

She shook her head as she let go of Ramone's hand and leaned back in the stiff chair. "I have no idea, but if I know him even a little, I know he will reach out to me. He never wants to lose control."

He reached into his desk and pulled out a business card. He took out a pen and wrote something down on the back and slid the card over to her. "Here is my private cell phone number. If you see him, you need to call or text me as quickly as possible."

She took the card and slipped it in her back pocket.

"For now, you can go. Collect your personal items from

the front desk. They will help you get a car or ride if you need one." Officer Ramone tried to smile, but his lips quaked with the unaccustomed movement. "And hey, I hope you know that everything I do is to keep my community safe. My arrest of you was nothing personal. I hope I don't have to ever do it again."

She stood up and brushed her hands over her hips. "It's my hope you never have to, either." She extended her hand. "If anything, I hope the next time I see you, you'll be telling me that you have Kelcie and Jackson and they're alive."

Chapter Nineteen

After collecting her personal items, Scarlett made her way down the white corridor leading out of the jailhouse. The place was quiet this late in the afternoon. Most people had gone home for the night, and as she walked her boots clicked on the tile and echoed through the open space. The sound made her nervous, though she couldn't explain why. Of all the places in the county, standing in the jail, where there were a myriad of cameras pointing at every possible corner, she reminded herself she was safe.

She of all people knew what an illusion safety really was. Safety couldn't even be found in the moments one spent alone in the comfort of their own home. The chaos of memories and the pain left in their wake had a way of creeping in, taking over and pulling off even the thickest scabs.

Her phone was running out of battery, but she had just enough charge to order a car. She was surprised Kalispell had an Uber service—some things about her former home state had changed for the better. Then again, its lack of amenities, tech and people were the reasons people left the cities and wanted to move to a place where it was gray and cold seven months of the year, and there was only about a three-week period when the weather was not too hot, cold or too smoky.

The place carried the scent of fear, stress and unwashed bodies. As it melded with the nervousness she felt, her pulse quickened, and a wave of sickness rose within her. The jail gave her the creeps.

The cold brass handles on the door were in sharp contrast to the heat of the summer evening as she stepped outside. The courthouse sat in the center of the city, the beige brick and stone building taking up the middle of a roundabout at the edge of downtown. It was ostentatious in its placement, as though the builder had chosen the spot so that the monument would stand as a constant reminder that the law would always be at the core of the town.

Unfortunately, thanks to its location, she had to stand outside the courthouse and watch as the constant stream of traffic passed by. Most people didn't seem to notice her as she watched the traffic, but some would rubberneck and stare at her like they were trying to figure out if she was a criminal or a courthouse employee.

She couldn't stand the looks of contempt.

Perhaps this was why the original city planner had placed the city center as they had—the public could focus on every possible criminal, and in doing so, they could act as judge, jury and executioner.

There was a grassy park across the street, the edges lined with maple and horse chestnut trees. In her summers as a kid, when her mother and father had come to the city for supplies, she and her siblings would make a game of picking up the spiny chestnuts and throwing them at one another. She still had a scar where one had stuck in her ribs like an angry porcupine and then got infected.

It was a silly memory, but it made her smile to think about one of the few fun memories she had with her brothers and sister. Most of the time they were fighting or spread out over the ranch, each taking care of the chores and tasks her father had used to keep them occupied.

A white pickup stopped for her as she waited at the sidewalk to cross the street toward the park. She barely looked as she gave the driver a quick wave of thanks and hustled across the road. When her feet touched the green lush grass she slowed, strolling beneath the lush canopies of the trees overhead. She picked up a horse chestnut and played with the spines with her thumbnail, as she thought about Cameron, the loss of Ben, Jamie and Wade.

When she got back to the ranch, she would have to see them. It was more than likely they'd already heard about her being back. Officer Ramone hadn't mentioned saying anything to Emily Trapper about her true identity, but between professional courtesy and her arrest record on the ranch, she was sure Emily had come to know her true identity.

Cameron had been far more kind than her other brothers, but he was still going to come at her with both barrels. She didn't know how much Ramone would have told Emily about what she had revealed to him, but she hated the thought of having to meet her brother and possibly her sister, Jamie, for the first time since coming back to Montana and confessing the drama that had followed her to their doorsteps.

If he told her to get out, she didn't know where she would go. She couldn't leave until she found Kelcie and Jackson. She had a man hunting her down, and the one man she wanted in her life had cast her out. If only she could call Miles and tell him how sorry she was for not having told him everything.

Their kiss haunted her.

He probably thought she was just using him and that she was nothing more than a two-bit actress who would manipulate anyone in her life in order to benefit herself. If he did, he probably wondered how she had caused the problems with Butch and what kind of relationship they had that would have caused him to feel so protective.

She stopped walking and put her hand on the coarse bark of a maple tree as emotions threatened to overtake her, though she didn't know why. Maybe it was that she had been through so much in such a short amount of time, or perhaps it was the thoughts of Butch and the loss of Miles, but she couldn't stop the tears from welling in her eyes and blurring her vision. They spilled over, and she let them stream down her cheeks as she leaned against the tree for support.

She hated being this emotional, but it felt cathartic to let all the fears and anxiety she had been feeling for so long fill her tears and pour down her face in hot rivulets. A sob rippled from her throat as she thought of Kelcie and what she could have possibly been facing—*if* she was still alive.

If she was dead, it was Scarlett's fault.

Her tears fell faster.

"Scarlett?" A man's hand grabbed her shoulder, and she jumped and turned.

Standing behind her was the overweight and graying Butch Hafner. He looked shorter and heavier than the last time she had seen him in New York. His hair was slightly mussed, like he had been running his fingers haphazardly through it while he had waited for her. His lips had sticky white saliva pooled in the corners, and the full effect of him made a chill run down her spine.

"What in the hell are you doing here?" she asked, her voice scratchy and weaker than she wanted.

She couldn't believe he had found her—and while she was crying, no less.

This is what came from allowing herself to feel. She had been so stupid.

"I've been waiting for you." He smiled, his teeth showing, and the effect reminded her of a growl. "That was nice of you to come alone." He took her by the arm and shoved her toward the road next to the park where a white truck with a grille guard was parked and running.

She jerked out of his grip. "Where is Kelcie?"

His smile turned to one of malice and hate. "If you were a better friend maybe she wouldn't have gone missing on your watch."

"You mean a *friend* like you?" she challenged, angrily wiping the tears off her cheeks with the back of her hand.

"I'm the greatest ally you've ever had. I *made* you who you are. You know I did and you know you owe me. You should be goddamned grateful."

He wasn't wrong. His ruthlessness in business had gotten her bumped to the front of casting lines, and his ability to feel nothing while negotiating had gotten her the best money, but that didn't mean she *owed him* anything. She wanted to tell him exactly that, but she needed to play it smart. She couldn't upset him any more. If she played along with him, he would bend. It was the only thing that had ever worked when dealing with him.

"I'll be grateful when you tell me where my friends are," she countered.

He laughed. "I bet you would. As soon as we get back home, I'll let them go."

"Home?" she asked, taken aback.

"Yes. *Our* home. I've been getting things ready ever since you said you wanted me."

She stopped. "When did I say I wanted you?" She knew she shouldn't have asked, that she should have just gone along with whatever it was he was saying, but she couldn't bear it.

"Don't you remember? It was when we were at dinner in Belarus. We were eating the fig and goat cheese pizza along the river. You told me you were glad to have me by your side, that you were happy, and you wanted me to work with you forever."

She didn't remember the conversation, but she did remember the wine they had been drinking. "I *did* want you to work with me..." *That was, until you had crossed the line*, she thought, proud of herself that she hadn't let it slip past her resolve.

"That's not all you want. I've always seen the way you look at me." He took her hand in his and pressed his cold fish lips against the back of her hand.

The feel of his skin was repulsive, but she did her best not to pull away. Instead, she moved inconspicuously for her phone. If only she had put Ramone's number directly in her phone, maybe she could have called him without Butch noticing.

"How do I look at you?" she asked, moving her pawn.

Butch took her hand again, stopping her from reaching for her phone. "You looked at me like you wanted to be the most powerful couple in Hollywood."

She hated him and the way his damp hand felt against hers. He disgusted her in the way his lip twitched when he smiled and how there was a thin sheen of sweat on the sides of his nose and over his brow. It reminded her of a man wanting sex, and her stomach turned.

He would never have her, no matter how *powerful* he thought they would be.

Her hand tightened around the horse chestnut she was still holding. The sea urchin-like spines poked into her hand like tiny needles, but the pain was reinvigorating and pulled her back from the disgust she felt from his touch.

"I'll do whatever you want if you just let Kelcie and Jackson go."

He glanced away and tilted his head back with exasperation. "Is that all you can think about right now? You haven't seen me in weeks, and you're only worried about *them*? Just get in my truck with me. We can talk all about your little friends in there." He motioned toward his running pickup.

"Are they okay? Unhurt?" she pressed.

"Don't worry about them." He turned his face away from her, making it impossible to read him.

There was something strange about his reaction to talking about Jackson and Kelcie, and it scared her. "You didn't hurt them, did you?"

"I'm not a monster, Scarlett."

She begged to differ. Normal people didn't track a person down across state lines and were so bold as to stalk them outside of a county courthouse filled with law enforcement.

He didn't care who saw him, like he thought he was smarter than anyone and above anyone's laws. The worst part is that she felt as powerless as he felt powerful.

She loosened her grip on the horse chestnut, and she glanced down at the spiky ball in her hand. There was only one way to take her power back. "Butch?" She said his name like it was a secret.

He shifted, and his brows rose with surprise and his eyes darkened with lust. "Yes, baby?"

"I hope you go to hell." She pulled her hand loose of his and swung wide, striking him hard in the side of the ribs.

"What in the—"

With the spiked chestnut in her palm, she slammed it squarely into his left cheek and eye.

He howled with pain as he grabbed at his eye. He swung his fist at her, wildly, connecting with her jaw, but she barely noticed.

The chestnut was lodged in his skin just under his eye.

He stepped back with pain, his body curling forward. She

pulled her hands into tight fists and bore down, striking him in the back, hard. The sound was hollow. He put his hand up as he cried out, gasping like he was searching for breath. But she didn't care.

She hated him.

She grabbed his shoulder as he took hold of her hips. Before he could stop her, she kicked her knee in his face with the sound of cracking bone. He let go, the place where he'd gripped hot with pain.

She turned and ran. His truck was running.

Not thinking, she ran to it, pulling at the door handle. It was open. Keys were in the ignition.

"You stupid cow!" Butch called from behind her, but she didn't turn to see if he was following.

All she could do was run away. She had to get away from this man. If he got his hands on her, she would never get away again.

"I will kill you!" Butch screamed.

She climbed inside the truck and locked the doors. Butch was stumbling toward her as she put the truck into Drive and skipped the tires as she slammed down the gas pedal.

As the truck tore off down the road, she heard a strange, dark sound. Looking in the mirror, she saw her contorted face. Inexplicably, she found that the mirthful sound was of her furious laugh.

Chapter Twenty

Officer Burns dropped Miles back at his truck outside the barn. The evening sun was bearing down, and he had chores to do. No matter what was happening in his personal life, he still had horses to feed. The animals depended on him, and unlike people, they were predictable.

He couldn't wrap his mind around the state of Jackson's apartment. If Burns was right and his brother had packed up in a hurry, that could only mean one thing—he had been behind Kelcie's disappearance. *If* that was the case, then the entire scope of their problems shifted. If he had taken her, the next question had to be whether or not Kelcie was going with him against her will.

He loved his brother, and though Jackson loved to drink and get a little Western on a Saturday night at The Mint Bar, Miles didn't think his brother was capable or motivated to commit such a crime.

Then again, he hadn't thought Scarlett was lying to him, either.

Maybe his ability to read people was the issue, and the people around him were far more nefarious than he had ever realized.

He walked into the barn and over to a stack of what was left from last winter's hay. It smelled of sweetgrass, alfalfa and dust. It was one of his favorite scents, reminding him of all the best parts of his life—sunshine, riding and the value of hard work.

It made him wonder what Scarlett's signature scent would have been—probably champagne and caviar. He stopped himself. He had been so wrong about her.

She was a Trapper. No matter how deeply she inserted herself in the world of actors and actresses, he had seen a spark of the real her when she had been riding. There was a cowgirl in her still.

The duality of her soul was one of the things he loved most about her. It was what had called to him before he'd even really given her any thought beyond that of her being a beautiful guest.

Yet, if she was such an actress, was it possible that she was trying to use this talk of a stalker and kidnapping of her assistant to get notoriety? People were always looking for insta-fame. He'd heard about it time and time again at the ranch. In fact, their marketing team at the Joy Luck had always talked about wanting to go viral. It was something they strove for but had never attained while he'd been working at that ranch.

He hated social media and the inanity of the beast. It was so fake and just a mask for the ugliness of life. People could put anything out there without fear of repercussions or reprisals. And, depending on how it was used, it could make a career, or end a life.

Scarlett had concealed her truth from him, and she had hidden painful parts of her past, but in hindsight he could understand why, and he could hardly blame her.

He plopped down onto a bale of hay and pulled out his phone. Looking up her social media accounts, he found no mention of anything that was going on at the ranch or in her personal life. The only thing she had posted in the last week was something about the show's upcoming episode.

It brought him a sense of relief.

Out of curiosity, he looked up the Joy Luck Ranch on Instagram. On their story were a series of pictures from last night's car accident on the ranch. They had used the hashtags #WestGlacierRanch, #DisasterRanch and #WreckAtTheRanch.

He couldn't believe it. What would possess the owners of the Joy Luck to post something so thoughtless? A man's life hung in the balance and a little boy could easily be left without a family, and these jerks were using it as a smear campaign against the ranch he worked for.

He had always known Drake Rex was a monster, but he hadn't known he would stoop this low.

Taking a quick screen shot, he sent a text of the image to Emily and Cameron, along with a simple question mark. They could make of it as they would, but they needed to be made aware of the smear campaign that was happening about the ranch.

If this was in direct response to his coming to work for the Trappers, he would have a bone to pick with Drake. The next time he saw the guy—they would have words.

Thinking about the accident and the Sullivans, Miles called up to the pediatrics floor at the hospital. A secretary answered the phone call on the second ring. "Pediatrics, this is Summer. How can I help you?"

"Hi, Summer, my name is Miles. I'm calling to check in on Thomas Sullivan. I was there with him last night. How is he doing today?" He was careful how he worded his question as to not raise any red flags or have the woman resist giving him information.

"He is doing well today. He'll be staying another night while he is on IV antibiotics, but I would think he will be able to go home in the next day or two."

"By chance, do you know how Aiden is doing?" He knew

he was pushing his luck, but he also knew how word spread in and around hospital staffers when families were involved in accidents like this.

"I'm sorry to tell you, but it sounds as though Aiden recently passed unexpectedly."

His heart broke for the kid.

"We attempted to contact his grandparents and other family members but have not been successful, thus far. If you could come in and help us with some paperwork, we would appreciate it. We currently need either a sworn statement or to get him assigned with a temporary guardianship if there are any decisions to be made."

"I'll be in as soon as I can," he said, though he had no idea how he would swing things in order to help the boy. "If things change, or he needs me in the meantime, please let me know."

"Will do, sir."

He hung up the phone, feeling more lost than he had before. Just when he thought he couldn't get more confused, something like this fell in his lap. There was no way he could take on the role of caring for a child—he barely had a job or a place to live. He wasn't stable enough to even consider caring for Thomas. He either had to find this boy's family or figure something out to help him—or hope the hospital could do something to help.

There was the sound of a truck racing down the drive, and it skidded to a stop outside the barn. Jamie must have been coming over to check on the horses or coming to ride her horse, Mac. Thankfully, there weren't supposed to be any more guests on the schedule until next weekend for the equine therapy program.

He stood up and shoved his phone in his pocket as he walked toward the front of the barn. "How's it going, Jamie?" he asked, before he stepped through the doors.

Instead of Jamie, he watched as a disheveled Scarlett stepped out of a white pickup with a dented grille guard on the front, one he didn't recognize, and slammed the truck door and stood there, lost. She looked frantic, and there was dried blood on her right hand. "Are you okay? What happened?" he asked.

She stared at him for a long moment, almost as though she didn't recognize him or couldn't make sense of where she was standing or what she was doing.

"Scarlett." He spoke her name softly. She didn't move. "Babe, it's okay." He eased toward her, walking slowly like she was a scared mare, and he was afraid she would bolt or start kicking.

He had no idea what had happened, but it had to have been traumatic, and it both frightened and infuriated him that he hadn't been there at her side.

She followed him with her eyes, but she said nothing as he drew nearer. He took the truck keys from her hand. "Whose pickup is this?" he asked, looking at the paper tag on the keys. It had PriceLess Rental Car Company printed on the ticket, along with a number.

Her gaze moved to the keys in his hands. "Oh." She sounded surprised and she stepped back, bumping into the truck. "I… I didn't mean to. I was just trying to get away. I'm going to be in so much trouble. Don't call the police."

"Slow down," he said. "Just start by telling me what happened." He put the keys in his pocket.

"I was coming out of the jail… Butch was waiting for me. He jumped me. I fought." She lifted her hands and turned her palms up.

There, on her right hand, were a series of bloodied pinpricks as though she had held a porcupine. "I hit him with a nut." She gave a strangled, victorious laugh.

"With what?" He couldn't have heard her correctly. "Did you kill him?"

She shook her head as she lowered her hands. "He's going to come for me. *Us.*"

He took out his phone and texted Emily, telling her about the attack outside the jail.

Her response was almost immediate:

I forwarded this to Ramone. Go to the CVA's office. Meet u there to help file a report.

"Do you know where he would have gone?" he asked.

She shook her head.

"Did he say anything about Jackson? Kelcie?"

Her eyes met his, and it was as though she was staring into the depths of his soul. "There was something about the way he talked about them. He was so...*vague*. It was unlike him."

"What do you mean?"

"I don't know... I can't be sure, but I don't know if he took them."

He understood what she said, but he couldn't make heads or tails of what she meant. If Butch hadn't taken his brother, they were back to the possibility that his brother was behind taking Kelcie—or someone else had taken them both. Yet, it didn't make sense.

Jackson didn't have any motivation for kidnapping Kelcie and then going absolutely silent.

His thoughts turned to the Joy Luck social media post about the accident. Would Drake have done something to his brother and Kelcie?

As ridiculous as Drake was, reveling in the tragedies of others and using it for personal gain, Miles couldn't imagine that he would orchestrate a kidnapping or potential murder. To do something like that was downright sociopathic.

They still had no idea where his brother and Kelcie were—and the more time that went by, the less likely they were to get them back.

"They want us to go to the crime victim advocate's office, and there we can file a police report about Butch's attack and also start the process of getting you a restraining order."

"They don't work." She shook her head, and her voice was weak, but he could tell by her tone that she was resigned to the idea.

"They may not, but I do. And come hell or high water, you aren't leaving my side again until we have this mess sorted out."

"Butch will stop at nothing to get to me. You don't understand."

He reached over to her and took her hands in his. She was trembling with fear. "I don't think *he* knows who he is dealing with, now. I will stop at nothing to make sure you are safe." He felt a sense of hypocrisy rise within him as he had promised her before that he would let nothing happen to her—and then he'd allowed Butch access. "And I'm sorry."

She tilted her head as she looked into his eyes. "What do you have to be sorry for?"

There were so many things, a litany. "I promised I wouldn't let him get to you. I should have been waiting for you at the jail. I should have been there when you needed me."

"You didn't know Ramone was going to cut me loose." She laced her fingers between his. "And I'm sorry for keeping my truth from you. I shouldn't have come here."

"This is where you were born and raised. Why do you think you shouldn't have come here?"

She dropped her gaze. "I told my father I'd never come back."

"That was your father. And from what I heard, your father was no peach." He paused. "But, if that's true, why *did* you come back?"

She sighed. "I told Butch how much I hated my dad, and we had talked about some of my memories as a kid. I thought that this would be the last place he would think of looking for me. He knows I wouldn't have wanted to come here—at least while my father was alive."

"Did he know your father passed?"

She shrugged. "He must have found out. And I have no idea how he tracked me here. I was careful to keep everything under wraps."

"Interesting." He had already hated the guy, but the thought of how deeply he had infiltrated her life made him hate him even more. If he saw him, he wasn't sure he would be able to refrain from becoming a monster.

Chapter Twenty-One

She must have looked like a disaster after meeting with the crime victim's advocate. The woman had been sweet and soft-spoken, asking Scarlett more questions than she wanted to answer, but getting every detail about Butch's attack outside the jail and even making sure to take pictures of the puncture wounds to her hands and sending them on to Emily.

Together, they made a quick call to Officer Ramone. He had been kind on the phone, gracious even, and there had been what almost sounded like relief in his voice when he'd heard she was in the office making a report.

As she made her way out of the small office, she found Miles sitting with Emily, and they were leaning toward each other and chatting quietly, looking conspiratorial. Seeing her, Emily stood up and sent her a caring smile. "Hi, Scarlett. Or should I say, sister?" she said, extending a welcoming hand.

She stopped mid-stride, her stomach instantly in knots. "I'm so sorry. I never meant to hurt anyone. I just—"

Emily stopped her with a raise of the hand. "You don't need to explain. I know all about your father, and I understand why you would have chosen to do what you've done in keeping your coming here a secret. As for you thinking I didn't recognize you… That's where you're wrong. I knew who you were from first time we saw each other." Emily gave a small laugh.

"What?" A profound sense of surprise and relief washed over her. "Why didn't you say anything?"

"Discretion is the better part of valor. If you wanted to be recognized and come in as family, you would have made it known." Emily smiled. "You're hardly the first person I've been around who wanted to keep things quiet." She pointed at the badge pinned to her chest.

"I appreciate your keeping things private. I was worried." She paused. "Did you tell my brother I'm here?"

Emily shook her head. "Miles and I've been talking about everything while you were in the office. I will contact your brother when I get home, if you're okay with it. In the meantime, we just need to make sure you are safe and protected. You don't need to worry about doing what you had to do. In the new generation of Trappers, we forgive, and we trust."

Of all the ways she thought it would go, this was the last.

"You really don't think Cameron is going to be upset? He hates me. I don't know if he told you, but the last time I saw him, we had a huge blowout."

Emily frowned. "What? If there was, he never mentioned it. If anything, your brother's super proud of you. He has been following your career and is always telling people about his famous sister."

She was embarrassed. After she had left in such a chaotic way, and with such bitterness in her heart, she would have never considered that her brother still cared about her, much less followed her career.

"I yelled at him when I left. There's no way he's not angry with me."

Emily put her hand on her shoulder, giving it a light and reassuring squeeze. "Who hasn't lost it on their brother at one point or another? I, personally, have raised my voice at your brother several times." She laughed. "You'd be surprised at the forgiveness that your brother is capable of. He's nothing like your father."

"I think my brother Ben was the most like him."

Emily nodded. "I'm sorry about his death, by the way. I'm sure it was hard on you, losing them both."

She tipped her head in acknowledgment. "I was surprised. I didn't think Ben was in so deep."

"It just goes to show you that you never really know who someone is. When a person is desperate, they will do almost anything to get what they want," Emily said, with a pinched expression as though she had seen that exact experience play out a million times.

Miles didn't seem able to meet her gaze, and Scarlett desperately wanted to talk to him and to keep apologizing for everything that had gone wrong between them from the moment she had set foot on the ranch. Yet, even if she did, she had the sinking sensation that he would still want nothing to do with her. She was nothing but trouble, and now she was also trouble with a capital *T*—as in Trapper.

Finally, he looked up as they neared the pickup. "You know, I've been thinking," he said, stopping. He leaned against the hood of the ranch truck. "When Butch came after you at the jail, did you get a good look at his hands and arms?"

She thought back. He'd been wearing a short-sleeve shirt. A button-up. Blue. Kind of preppy and out of style. Jeans that looked like something he'd bought at a high-end boutique on Rodeo Drive, but were really for men twenty years younger than he pretended to be.

"I don't know." She could only think about how it had both hurt and freed her to shove the impromptu weapon into his face. "Why?"

He tapped his fingers on the hood, making a hollow sound that echoed down the alley behind the indistinct white building that held the CVA's office. "I'm just thinking about the blood we found at the cabin. If he was the one who broke in—and if that's where he took them—then he would have some kind of cut on his arm. Right?"

"You're right," Emily said, pointing to him. "We did collect a few fingerprints on scene." Her fingers tapped on her phone, and she didn't even look up. "I'm going to have my team at the lab run them against Butch's and see if anything matches there."

"What if they don't?" Scarlett asked.

Emily looked up. "Why do you ask that? Do you really think that someone else could have been behind the break-in and kidnapping?"

She didn't know what had made her ask. Maybe it was fear. "I just… I don't know. I guess I just can't imagine Butch breaking a window. He's kind of a wimp."

"A wimp who tried to kidnap you outside of a county courthouse," Emily countered.

"Touché."

"I want you to text him." Emily lifted her phone. "Ask him for proof of life of both Jackson and Kelcie."

"Don't you think he would wonder what was up if I asked for that?"

Miles tipped his head as though in agreement.

"Call it whatever you want when you talk to him. Just say you want to know what he's asking for to get them back. And before you agree to anything, say you need proof they are safe." Emily went back to her phone. "I'm going to call in reinforcements."

"You're assuming he doesn't sniff us out."

Emily tipped her head in acknowledgment. "He may, but I'm thinking he has his hands full in trying to get a new rig. You took his truck. How is he getting around? I'm going to get my guys to watch the local taxi and car services. If we watch, he may lead us directly to our missing persons."

That was, if they got lucky. So far, luck had never had a presence in Scarlett's life.

"Text him," Emily said, motioning toward Scarlett's phone.

Scarlett's hands were shaking as she clicked on the screen. She typed:

I want my friends back, but first I need proof they are okay.

Not waiting, she sent another quick message.

Send me a pic.

The message was marked Read. Then a series of dots showed up on her screen, letting her know that Butch was typing. They stopped, then started again as though he was thinking about what he was typing, deleting and typing something out instead.

Did you think you could hurt me and get away with it?

Her breath caught in her throat.

Kelcie will pay for what you did to me.

He wouldn't hurt Kelcie. Not if he really wanted to be with her. If he hurt her best friend, there was no way she could ever forgive him. He had to have known that. She sent a message.

Don't you dare! Don't lay a finger on her. If you want me to play your game, you have to play by my rules.

The message was marked Read, but he didn't respond.

She waited, hoping he would send a picture. Nothing came. No three dots. No indication he was typing. He was angry—and more, now he was truly dangerous as he was more unpredictable than ever.

You're kidding yourself, Scarlett. You play by mine.

Emily stepped beside her, reading the texts from over her shoulder. She sucked in a breath and reached for the phone, motioning for her to hand it over.

Scarlett hesitated, unsure whether or not to trust the woman, but she had no other options. Her sister-in-law was the greatest weapon she had in this war. Her fingers moved fast as she typed.

Show me Kelcie and Jackson. Now.

A minute later a picture arrived.

They said a picture was worth a thousand words. This picture was so much more, but less, and in a singular word—sickening.

Kelcie's face was black and blue, her left eye was a purple so dark it bordered on black, and it was swollen shut. On her eyebrow was a large cut where she must have taken some kind of blunt object to the face.

There was another cut like it on her cheek on the other side of her face, below her eye, and blood seeped from the cut and had dried in a long brown crusted river. Her hair was still in the same ponytail Scarlett had seen her wearing but it was pulled into patches that had come loose and now lay limp against her neck. Below the hairs on her neck were scratch marks and well-defined red and purple fingermarks as though Butch had tried to strangle her at some point.

She was tied to a chair, and behind her, there was the back of what she assumed was Jackson's head. His hair was dark and matted with dried blood. His head was drooped down like he was sleeping or had lost consciousness.

Show me Jackson's face.

Emily texted, obviously as concerned about the man as Scarlett.

A moment later, a picture came through. His eyes were closed and there was dried blood at the corner of his lip and under his nose, none was fresh. Jackson's head was tilted sideways and back, his mouth slightly open as if he was snoring—or dead.

Emily tapped away on the phone.

Where do you want me to meet you? When?

There were the dots. Then more dots. Then nothing.

They waited for five minutes. They were the longest minutes of her life—each felt like an hour of sitting on a fire ant hill, each ticking second a stinging bite to her soul.

Still there was no answer.

Emily sighed. She sent pictures of the texts to her phone and then handed Scarlett back her cell phone. "I let Ramone know what is happening. He recommended that we move you to a safe location until we have this situation under control. Would you be willing to go into hiding?"

"What does that mean?" She looked at Miles. She wouldn't leave him.

"We have agreements with some of the local hotels. We will get you a room where you can stay as long as you need." Emily smiled as she seemed to pick up on the way Scarlett silently pleaded with Miles for help. "And Miles is welcome to remain with you, should you wish."

For the first time since she had stepped foot in Montana, Scarlett finally felt the knot in her gut loosen. She was no longer fighting alone—she had law enforcement and Miles at her side. She needed to pay attention, but thankfully they didn't think she was crazy, and now Butch was no longer just a shadow lurking at the corner of her nightmares.

Chapter Twenty-Two

Miles was only too happy to see Emily get back into her rig outside of the Hilton Garden Inn in Kalispell after she had followed them there and set them up in an adjoining room suite. Though no one had said anything, the door between his room and Scarlett's wasn't going to be closed—not as long as he had a damned thing to say about it. He'd made her a promise and he was standing by it. He wasn't leaving her alone again, not when there was a stalker on the loose.

Scarlett stood at his side in front of the lobby doors of the hotel. The awning was overhead, blocking the moon but casting long, dark shadows across their faces thanks to the fluorescent lights installed overhead.

The hotel was nice by Montana standards, with its slate and river rock aesthetic, but he doubted that it compared to anything that Scarlett was used to—that was at least now that she had escaped this world and become established in her new California persona. Rustic was a far cry from the marble and gold encrusted world of the rich and famous.

Then again, she had come back. This is where she had run to when she needed help. There was power and unquestionably something unchained in this Western world. This was the place in America where people came to free their hearts and untether their souls—even if that meant unburdening themselves of their enemies in the process, no matter what that process entailed.

If this unburdening included Butch's death, Miles had to admit he would be only too happy to pull the trigger if the man put Scarlett's life at risk. Miles would stop at nothing to keep her safe.

Almost as if the deputy could read the thoughts on his face, she scowled. "I don't want you to do anything stupid while you two are here. Do you hear me? You are here as a representative not only of the ranch, but of my family, as well. Okay, Miles?"

She seemed to have forgotten that it was his brother sitting next to Kelcie in the picture Butch had sent, as well. Scarlett wasn't the only one hurting and afraid, but he wasn't about to point it out. Silence was his best play.

He answered with a simple nod.

She looked at Scarlett. "I set up your phone to forward anything from Butch directly to my team. Anything you send to him will also be mirrored to our systems."

"Are you monitoring everything on my phone?"

"If I have your consent, I'd like to."

Scarlett opened her purse to pull out her phone and stared inside for a long moment before reaching in and grabbing it. "Here."

"Oh," Emily said, waving her off, "we don't actually need it. We can do everything remotely. We have the ability to access. I just needed your okay."

He would have been lying if the invasion into her privacy didn't make him just the tiniest bit uncomfortable. It wasn't that he didn't know everything on every digital device was like a giant open source of information to anyone who was the slightest bit technically savvy, but he was just so far from adept at that side of life that he'd liked to stick his head in the sand.

For some reason, it made his thoughts move back to the trail cameras when he'd taken Scarlett, Kelcie and the Sullivans on the mountain. It was almost laughable to think how annoyed he'd been to have them looking into their activities, when anyone in the world could have been doing basically anything they wanted to be doing on the tiny devices that each one of them had along with them in their pockets and purses.

Privacy and anonymity were truly nothing more than an illusion in the modern world.

Scarlett dropped her phone back into her purse. "I know this is a horrible question, given everything that is going on, but my wallet..."

Emily's eyes darkened and she tapped on her chin. "Oh, yes... I bet you are missing that. Do you know how your wallet would have come to be found under the master bedroom's bed? I know you told Ramone that you hadn't been in the cabin and that you didn't realize it was missing, but do you know the last time you had seen it?"

Scarlett shrugged. "I told Ramone that the last time I know for sure was when I had it hanging in the barn while we were getting the horses ready to go. I remember it hitting against my perfume bottle. Oh, wait..." She gasped and opened her purse wide. "I just now realized, my perfume bottle is missing, too. It's a bottle of YSL. I always carry it with me."

He couldn't see where her missing a bottle of perfume would have a bearing on what was happening, but it was a strange thing to have been gone from her things.

"And did you see anyone you didn't know while you were getting ready to go?" Emily asked.

She shook her head. "It was just us. Kelcie, Miles and me."

"No Butch?"

"I didn't see him, but that doesn't mean he wasn't somewhere."

That was the thing about stalking, a person could have been in any corner. If the stalker was good, a person wouldn't even have a clue they were being watched.

He sent Emily a look. "Maybe it's time we talk about putting some cameras up around the ranch."

She answered with a stiff nod. "Don't think that hasn't already crossed my mind." She tapped her fingers on the steering wheel. "Go get in your rooms. If you need anything, charge it to the room or keep receipts. We will cover your expenses, but keep it between the mustard and the mayonnaise." She gave him a sly smile.

"You got it, boss." He chuckled.

"I'll sit out here for a bit and make sure that no one comes or goes that shouldn't. I also have talked to the hotel staff. They know no one is to go to or from your room that is not associated with law enforcement or the hotel staff. If you need anything, call."

"Thank you for everything, Emily," Scarlett said. Her voice sounded scratchy and heavy with emotions. It was so thick, he reached over to her and pulled her hand into his.

"I've got this under control for now." He put his entwined hands on Scarlett's lower back and turned her toward the door. He gave Emily a slight two-fingered wave as they made their way into the hotel and out of sight.

It shouldn't have brought him any relief to leave his boss, but perhaps it was because he was once again alone with Scarlett that he felt a sense of peace. He'd wanted this moment for a while now. He needed to know she was really okay. He needed her to know she was safe and cared for as long as she was with him, even if nothing ever happened between them.

Not that he wouldn't have wanted something to happen… He certainly would.

They made their way to the top floor and down to the end of the hall where their suite waited. Considering the Flathead County Sheriff's Office had put them up, he was impressed. He would have expected something at the hourly rate motel at the edge of town, not at the best place in town and in the nicest room. Emily must have really been trying to make good with her newly minted sister-in-law.

He couldn't blame her—he was trying to make up for a few things himself.

Scarlett waited for him to scan the room key to let her in, and he followed her inside, not missing his opportunity to check out her perfectly fitted jeans and the view they created from behind. His hand twitched as he thought about how badly every part of him wanted to reach out and touch her round behind.

This woman drove him to the brink of glorious madness, but at the same time she was all the most beautiful parts of life. She was adventure, chaos, passion, emotions and a hunger for life all wrapped up into the most stunning woman he'd ever seen. He could imagine no more perfect woman on the planet—especially for him.

There was only a handful of issues that held him back. All of them were massive on their own, but none of them were completely insurmountable.

He closed the door behind them, then made his way through both suites, clearing them. Nothing had been disturbed since Emily had gotten them the rooms and done a quick walkthrough. They were safe—or, at least, as safe as they could be with a stalker trying to get to the woman he loved.

Wait. Did he *love* her?

He stopped moving, pretending to stand at the edge of the curtain and stare out the window, which looked out onto the city center.

Her footfalls sounded as she moved on the hardwood floor toward him. She put her hand on him, making heat rise from the place where her fingers grazed against his skin. "Is everything okay?"

He nodded, afraid that if he actually spoke his voice would crack and everything he was thinking and feeling would come spilling out like some wave of unchecked flotsam.

She didn't need his chaos to add to the upheaval happening in her personal life. If she wanted him, she could make that choice, but he couldn't be the one to make a move.

"I appreciate you being here." She moved beside him and under his arm, pushing her body against him and making his heart race. "You kept your word to me. After everything that has happened, you don't know how much that means to me. I know I didn't earn your loyalty, and I most certainly don't deserve it, but I'll do everything to show you that you were right in placing it with me."

"I don't know why you're being so hard on yourself, Scarlett," he said, making sure not to let go of her as he turned ever so slowly to face her. "You did what you had to do to keep yourself and your friend safe."

She looked down. "But I failed."

"You didn't fail. You did what you could. You got here. You came to a place you knew people would help you."

"But I didn't know for sure."

He lifted her chin gently with his finger. "Look at me. I'm up here."

There were hints of tears in her eyes. "You did know. You knew exactly what kind of people you would find here at the ranch now that your father is gone. You can fight and bicker, but your family will always support you, and so will the people that they have invited into their lives, like me."

"You say that now, but there was no way I was to know that. I haven't even seen Cameron yet. Plus, the last time I saw them, I had them all lumped up together as my father's flying monkeys. I didn't think there was much of a chance that I would come back here to open arms. Emily's reception of me was a huge surprise—one I'm exceptionally grateful for." She looked at him like she was weaving herself into him. "And I'm so thankful for you."

He leaned in and found her lips waiting for him. The world around them disappeared into a flurry of moving hands and clothing being pulled and unbuttoned and unzipped. She threw his hat onto the counter of the kitchenette, and she stopped for only a brief second as she looked at his belt buckle.

"That's beautiful. Yours?" she asked, pulling it open.

He shook his head. "Grandfather's."

"Nice." She kissed him again as he moved out of his pants, and she followed suit.

They moved toward the bed, his hands tracing over the lines of her expensive-looking black lace bra and panty set. It didn't escape him what kind of woman she was, and how lucky he was, that he had found a woman who could live through a day straight from the pits of darkness and still look like she had fallen from the beauty of the stars.

He lifted her into his arms, working her hard nipple through the thin fabric of her bra with his mouth as she wrapped her legs around his waist. She gasped as she ran her fingers through his hair and pulled tight. The edge of pain made him nip, running his teeth against her hardness.

She pulled his head up and devoured his kiss. He moved her against the wall beside the bed, pressing her back against the cold sheetrock as he let his hand move down to her breast. He cupped her flesh, feeling the full roundness of her in his palm. Every part of her was perfect for him, with all of its dimples and tiger stripes from its formation and growth.

He ran his tongue along the line of a fine, faded and silvered stretch mark on the top of her breast, and she moaned. He basked in the salty flavor of her vanilla-scented skin.

"Miles, I want you. Now," she begged, her breath filling his mouth, and he breathed her in.

The sensation of taking her into him like that was so sensual and sexy that it made him grow impossibly harder.

Sex had always been important to him—in that way he was different than a lot of other dudes he knew. It was about emotion. He had to connect with a woman, and really connect, not just on superficial nonsense, to want to take things here.

Now that they were crossing this bridge, and she was in his arms, the last thing he wanted to do was not make it last. He needed to slow his roll.

He leaned back and looked into her eyes, studying her in the thin light cast from the moon peeking through the window. "Do you know how exceptionally beautiful you are?"

She smiled, and there was a sparkle in her eyes as she met his gaze. "And do you know how handsome you are?" She tilted her head ever so slightly as she tightened the grip of her thighs around his waist. "You are one of the main reasons I came here. I saw you…and I knew."

He kissed the mark on her breast softly, letting his exhalation caress the wetness he'd left on her skin before casting his gaze back up upon her. "What did you know?"

"I knew…" There was a moment of hesitation, and she tried to cover it up with a sweet kiss to his lips before she released her legs from him and slipped down.

Part of him wanted her to say that she loved him, too. Yet,

he was afraid that if she did, this would all be too real and even more dangerous than it already had become. She was going to break his heart, that was a known, but to have this one night with her was worth all the heartbreak in the world. She was his Aphrodite.

He longed for the words to fall from her lips, but he feared them just as much.

"I knew," she finally continued, in what felt like hours later, "that I would be *safe* with you."

Safe was a hell of a long way from love. In fact, it lived on the opposite ends of the universe.

Both words carried such weight that he wasn't sure which he feared more—and yet, in his heart for a fleeting moment, he realized that in a just and right world, safety could only be brought through the bounty of love.

She sat down on the bed and pushed his boxers down to the floor in one swift motion. A small squeak escaped her lips as she stared at his wanting body. He wasn't sure what to make of her noise until she looked up at him, took hold of him and sent him a wide smile.

"I knew I was lucky, but I had no idea exactly how lucky I was going to get tonight." She laughed, moving her hand down his length.

"Oh…" He moaned. "I'm the lucky one." He pushed her down onto the bed and moved between her naked thighs. He found her wetness and let his tip press ever so slightly against it, teasing her with what was to come. "Tonight, we're going to let 'er buck, baby."

She wrapped her legs around him and lifted her body as he drove inside of her, making her gasp. "Oh, my… Miles." She said his name like each letter was its own syllable, and he moved his body with the sounds.

He would give anything to make the sounds she was making and the sensations she was making him feel last forever.

Scarlett's body pressed against him, her breasts damp with sweat and her hard nipples pressing against his chest.

He flipped her over in one swift motion, not letting his body slip from her. Her eyes were wide with excitement and thrill as she laughed and moved to sitting atop him.

The motion of her hips came naturally, flowing and ebbing, rounding and striking like waves cascading and crashing with the tides of ecstasy.

Her body quickened and the round circling of her hips became more focused and driving. The expression on her face changed to one of beautiful concentration as she held her breath, and the wave he'd been hoping to help her catch took her away.

She collapsed onto his chest for a moment, her heart hammering against his, but she smiled at him with the glazed expression of a satisfied woman who was far, far from sated.

He was going to be in for one hell of a ride.

Chapter Twenty-Three

Last night had been the best night of her life. Hands down. It was complex and deep, soft and compassionate. Yet, there was a brevity and lightness to it that Scarlett's heart had desperately needed.

There were so many things she appreciated in Miles, and as much as she wanted to tell him that she loved him last night, she was glad she hadn't taken that leap.

If he had been paying attention, though, her body would have already told him everything. She had given him everything she'd ever wanted to give to a man and feelings within her that she had not even known she was able to give.

She looked up at his sleeping face. He looked so at peace. The thought of ever leaving this place, this room, his arms, made her body ache.

There had been men in her life before, but she had never felt as she did in this moment. It was as if he held the power to make every horrible thing, every memory and every fear simply disappear. He was the one thing she had always been searching for, and now that she had finally found him, the last thing she wanted to do was go back to the nightmares of their shared reality.

She snuggled deeper into the nook of his arm and laid her head down on his chest and watched as it rose and fell with the comfort of sleep. He was tanner than she would have expected, and he had visible muscles even when he was sleeping. She was used to men who worked out—the men on set were usually the kinds who counted each individual gram of protein and took every supplement known to mankind, but they didn't have bodies that compared.

Miles's body was the kind that came from real hard work and long days spent taking care of the needs of the ranch and its guests. She could only guess how many bales of hay he moved in a day and how many saddles he put on and took off.

The thought of him manhandling the leather saddles made her have a flashback of her running her fingernails down the perfect curves of the muscles of his back last night. He had smelled so good, and the way he moved when he worked to pleasure her… She would give anything to feel him between her thighs every day for the rest of her life.

If only she could be so lucky.

He was a rugged ranch man, and she was a city girl.

What kind of future could their love have?

Right now, that was the last thing she wanted to waste time or energy thinking about. Instead, she lazily ran her fingertip down the chiseled line at the center of his abs. He was so damned hot.

He shifted under her touch, and she smiled, thinking about what they could do if she woke him up with just the right amount of grazing fingertips.

Miles opened his eyes, squinting as he gazed down at her. "You are playing with fire, princess." His voice was sexy and rough from the ravages of a night spent in the throes of ecstasy and the exhausted sleep that followed.

"Oh? Am I? I thought I was provoking a stallion, cowboy." She giggled.

"Whatever you want to call it, but if you aren't careful,

you're going to be riding me until you can't walk." He sent her a devilish grin.

"I hope that's a promise." As it was, staying in bed with him was the only place she really wanted to be.

For all intents and purposes, they were in protective custody until further notice, which meant until they heard otherwise—what had he said to her last night? She could *let 'er buck.*

She moved her hand lower, but just as she did, there was a hard knock on the hotel room door.

Miles jumped from the bed and hurried out of her bedroom and to his own as if their shared bed had been electrified. His sudden departure unexpectedly hurt, but she didn't quite know why—perhaps it was because it carried an air of possible embarrassment of his being seen with her in such a compromising position, or maybe it was that he seemed so well practiced at running.

The knocking sounded again.

"Who is it?" she called.

There was only a muffled sound from the hallway. Whoever had knocked probably couldn't hear her any better than she could hear them.

Grabbing her clothes, she pulled them on. She wiggled her jeans up her leg, hopping as she slipped them the last bit of the way up and pulled closed the zipper. Her hair had to have been a mess, and she gave it a quick brush with her fingers and then pulled it back into a messy bun as she stepped to the door.

Clicking open the bar lock, she flipped open the cylinder and then opened the door. She expected to find Emily standing there in her black uniform, her standard resting cop face in place, but instead there was a woman in blue jeans, a brown button-down shirt and a straw cowboy hat that was dirty around the crown from sweat and dust. The cowgirl was about her age, maybe a bit younger, but her skin carried extra years thanks to sun and wind.

The woman weighed and measured her messy bun, disheveled clothes and sockless feet and found her wanting. She moved to push past her.

"Can I help you?" Scarlett asked, standing her ground.

The woman gave her a look that could have nearly been deadly. "I know who you are and exactly what the hell you have been up to, you harlot. Get out of my way."

The woman's fiery outburst made Scarlett laugh, the sound coming unexpectedly and from deep in her core. Given all the things that had happened in the last week to her, this woman's pitiful show of strength was the least of her concerns. "I'm doing no such thing—and as much as you seem to know who I am, I can't say I know a thing about you. So, unless you want me to call the police, you better turn your country ass around and head out from whatever rathole you climbed out of." Scarlett pointed toward the hall.

The woman's scowl deepened, and her hands balled tightly. Scarlett saw the punch coming a second before the woman's fist even started to arc wildly through the air. Reaching up, she grabbed the woman's arm with her left hand, and the cowgirl yelped with shock and anger. The woman punched with her left, connecting weakly with Scarlett's ribs.

"What in the hell?" Scarlett cried, letting go of the woman's arm and pushing her away and into the metal doorjamb with a loud *thump.*

"What's going on?" Miles called from behind her.

She turned as Miles stepped out of the door connecting their suites. He was slipping his white T-shirt on over his head, and he stopped mid-stride. The woman behind her grabbed a fistful of her hair and yanked, hard, sending her reeling backward.

Scarlett spun on her heel, her right fist instinctively flying and connecting with the woman's gut. The woman let out a grunting wheeze but didn't let go of her hair. Scarlett swung again, full on facing her this time as she lunged toward the woman. Her fist connected with the woman's cheek so hard it made pain run down her hand and into her arm.

The woman's hand relaxed, and Scarlett pulled herself loose of the woman's grasp and stepped back into Miles's arms. "Chloe? What in the hell?" He moved Scarlett behind him, giving her a quick once-over as if making sure there was no blood drawn. "Are you all right, babe?"

Scarlett smiled wildly. "That cowgirl picked a fight with the wrong Trapper."

"Don't think you're tough just because you got the drop on me. I was playing nice," Chloe called, leaning around Miles like she was looking for another round.

"Come at me," Scarlett jabbed. "We both know the only thing you are good at is picking the wrong man." She laughed, well aware she was kicking the hornet's nest, but she wasn't afraid of any potential sting.

Chloe lunged, but Miles stopped her with one hand. "Don't you dare." He stepped into her, moving her farther out of the room and now fully into the hallway. "Why are you here, Chloe?" He peered around, but it appeared as though she was alone.

"Drake sent me."

"Your new boy toy?" Miles's voice was darker than Scarlett had ever heard, and it tore at her heart.

"He is more of a man than you'll ever be," Chloe said with a near growl.

"If that was true, he wouldn't have sent you to do his job," Scarlett countered.

"You need to go." Miles moved to close the door in her face, but Chloe moved her foot into the doorjamb and stopped him.

"If you think I wanted to be here, you're stupid. This was our attempt at an olive branch so maybe you'd lay off stealing any more business. If you want to be a jerk, so be it—we can play dirty. We just thought you'd want to know we heard about what was happening and we have a line on your brother."

Miles pushed the door wide open.

Scarlett couldn't have been more surprised if the woman had sprouted wings and started to fly around the room like a sparrow.

"Don't trust her, Miles." Scarlett searched his face to see if he was tempted to actually believe the woman.

His expression softened and Scarlett panicked. She moved to touch him.

"Don't listen to your new piece of ass, Miles. If you had answered your phone, I wouldn't have just shown up like this, but you've been ignoring me. If anything, my being here is a sign you *can* trust me."

Scarlett sent Miles a questioning glance, and he sighed in acknowledgment. She couldn't be mad that he'd failed to mention anything about his ex-girlfriend reaching out.

"How did you get past the cops and the hotel security? They are supposed to be watching the rooms," Scarlett asked, a new fear rising within her at how easily this strange woman had been able to get access after Emily had promised them anonymity and safety.

"My cousin Amber works here. She knew I was trying to get in touch with Miles. She helped me get in and bypass people. Don't be mad at her. She knew this was important."

Chloe gave Miles a pleading look. "You remember her. You liked her."

Miles nodded. "Okay, Chloe. But why exactly did you come here? You can't say you care about me or my family."

"You and I both know you and I were never going to work out as a couple. I went about it all wrong, and I shouldn't have acted the way I did, but I loved someone else. Life happens. That doesn't mean I hate you or your brother. I don't want to see him get hurt."

Scarlett hated the woman, there was no question about those feelings, however she wasn't sure whether or not the woman was telling Miles the truth. If anything, she almost felt like an interloper in a life that predated her, and it made her hate the woman even more.

Then again, she had to give her a modicum of respect for trying to bridge the gap between right and wrong by keeping her former lover's brother safe.

That didn't mean they would ever be friends.

"Well, I appreciate your reaching out. I do." Miles ran his hand over the back of his neck in discomfort. "I'm surprised you'd want to help, but..."

"I've never hated you, Miles."

"And I've..." he started, but there was hesitation in his attempt to return the sentiment.

"It's okay. I deserved it. I didn't treat you right. And I sure as hell shouldn't have called and threatened you. I was just pissed when I saw y'all on our trail cameras." Chloe sighed. "I'm sorry."

"I appreciate the apologies," Miles said.

Scarlett turned and walked into her room. The cowgirl could have her minute—she'd paid her black-eye toll. It would never be enough, in her humble opinion, but if the woman hadn't fumbled the handsome Miles, then Scarlett wouldn't have landed him—so really, she was the true winner in every way.

Scarlett pulled her bed together. It was a little petty, but she couldn't help but leave it somewhat imperfect as a hint of what had transpired last night. Miles had come out on top in life, and they were the winners.

Chloe cleared her throat. "That's what brought me here… The cameras. I called the police department, but they gave me the runaround when I told them who I was. I think they took me about as seriously as Scarlett there," she said, motioning toward her. "Can't say I blame any of them, but I'd like to think you know me better than that. I'm not a total piece of garbage."

She still couldn't come to terms with trusting the woman, no matter how much she tried to convince Miles to the contrary.

"Where did you see Butch taking Jackson and Kelcie?" Miles asked.

"Who's Butch?" Chloe asked, frowning. "I just saw Jackson on the cameras with Kelcie. She was hiking with him on the south trails—not far from where you guys went up. She had her arm wrapped up in a sling? Black bandana. Walked with a limp."

"Wait. What?" Scarlett asked, walking back and facing the woman. "What were they doing? Did you hear what they were talking about?"

It didn't make sense. Butch had them. He'd told her that he had them. He was in Kalispell. He was stalking her. He was holding them over their heads.

"I don't know. The cameras only take stills every thirty seconds or so. They're not videos. Not what we do." Chloe reached into her pocket and pulled out a folded note. "Here are the GPS coordinates of the last spot we saw them on the trail cams. We sent the cops the same. I hope this can be of some help. From here on out, we want you to shut down the guest services side of the West Glacier Ranch. You can keep the JMac Therapy going."

Miles took the piece of paper and, opening it, studied it for a long moment. "I can't make any kind of deals with you, but I'll talk to my bosses. Your help will go a long way in a healthy working relationship moving forward."

"If you need anything else from us, you know how to get in touch." Chloe stepped out of the room. "And good luck getting your brother and your friend back," she said, motioning toward Scarlett.

"Yeah, thanks," Scarlett said, half embarrassed and not quite sure how to feel. "Sorry about the fireworks."

Chloe nodded. "Me, too."

Miles closed the door and turned toward Scarlett. "If this is below where we rode in, I think I know exactly the trail where we can find them."

"Is there a house there or something? How did Butch send us a picture of them tied up? How did he get that kind of image?" Scarlett couldn't put the pieces together. It just didn't make sense.

Miles shook his head. "There's a house back there. It's small. Maybe they're in there. And for all we know, maybe he just didn't show up on the trail cameras. It's possible he was just out of the frame."

There was also the sickening possibility that she had been wrong all along, or that this disappearance had just gotten a whole lot more complicated.

Chapter Twenty-Four

Miles nudged Oreo forward, making sure that Seagrass, Mac and the rest of the string of horses and their riders were following behind him. Scarlett had been off ever since Chloe had shown up at their hotel room, but he could hardly blame her. No one was supposed to have been able to have access to them—and then bam, the one person he never thought he'd have to deal with showed up on their doorstep.

He had hated her over the last few months because of what she had done to him and how their relationship had ended, but it had taken some gumption for her to come to him with what she had found on their trail cameras. There was still some niggle of doubt that she was to be trusted. Chloe had rarely done anything that didn't serve her own selfish purposes first and foremost. Her reaching out was to attempt to gain leverage for Drake. Which was where Miles's greatest hang-up lay.

The coordinates she'd given him did line up with the old miner's cabin in the woods, though. It would have been a perfect location for someone to hide out or to post up with hostages. Which was the next major obstacle and question they faced—was this a kidnapping, or was this all somehow staged?

Who was really behind Jackson and Kelcie's disappearance? If Butch was involved, how and why?

There were very few who knew about the abandoned cabin. It was utilized by Forest Service workers, backcountry hikers and trail riders. It was comprised of nothing more than a couple of bunks and a small kitchen area. Outside there was a latrine, frost-freeze spigot and water trough for folks who stopped with horses.

For years, it had been known only to a handful of people and the local ranches when they ranged cattle in the high country. Between Jackson, Kelcie and Butch, only Jackson would have known that place had existed.

Which meant his brother could have played a role in this kidnapping and ransom attempt.

Emily was at the back of the string with officers Ramone and Burns. They were talking quietly amongst themselves, but from snippets of their conversation he had been able to pick up since they had left the barn, they had been just as confused by the events that had transpired as he was.

When he'd told them about the coordinates of the possible location of Jackson and Kelcie, he'd made sure to leave out the part about Chloe stopping by their hotel room to hand them off. Instead, he'd left it vague in an attempt to keep her from getting in trouble. If she had been doing them a favor, then he didn't want to cause her problems—but if she was lying, he would be the first one to throw her under the bus.

Scarlett rode up beside him. "Do you think that they are going to be there when we arrive?"

The concern that they would already be somewhere else had crossed his mind. "I don't know, but we need to start somewhere. Chloe didn't say she had pictures of them coming out, so we have to hope that they only went in."

"If they never came out…" She sent him a pained expression.

"Kelcie's still alive. She's going to be okay. If Butch wants you and his money, the last thing he would do is kill her." *Jackson, on the other hand…*

He swallowed back the bile rising in his throat. His brother would be okay. Sure, the only pictures they'd gotten of him since he'd been held for ransom were of him completely incapacitated, but that didn't mean he was dead.

Scarlett slipped her hand into his as they made their way along the trail, as though she could sense his fears. They were in this together.

"Scarlett?" He spoke her name like it was a question.

"Yes?" she asked, clenching his hand as she smiled at him.

"No matter what happens out here today, you are safe with me. I hope you know that."

"I know," she said, but there was a strain in her voice, and she let go of his hand and nudged her horse forward.

He wanted to tell her that he loved her and he would take a bullet for her—literally or figuratively. But from that tone, he wasn't sure she would believe him, and it definitely wasn't the time or the place. He didn't need to make things more confusing for either of them.

Ahead the trail zigzagged and dropped down. It would level out and from there they would drop into the small valley where there was the cabin, a log corral and a hayshed. Normally, he would take the horses right in and tie them up or corral them and give them some water, and this group of animals knew the drill.

They started to head down the trail, unbidden. Seagrass was in the lead, and it made his thoughts turn to Thomas and the last time they had been riding together. The memory made him smile, but it also made him realize exactly how much had transpired in such a short amount of time. It was no wonder his emotions were so raw and he felt as he did toward Scarlett. They had gone through a lifetime's worth of drama in a blink of an eye, and their bond was something that would never be broken—at least, if he had anything to say about it.

He gave a low whistle to Scarlett, and she turned to look at him. He motioned for her to stop and pointed toward a thicket of trees. He moved Oreo off the trail and led the way toward where he'd shown her. The officers behind them followed.

As he got down, he tied up and helped the others. Emily and Scarlett were good on their own, but the other two were soup sandwiches as they got off. Ramone walked stiffly toward him, half hunched like he hadn't been in a saddle in twenty years.

Ramone cleared his throat. "So, I want you and Scarlett to stay with the horses here. We don't need things going sideways and you getting hurt. You hear me?"

There wasn't a chance in hell that he was going to let Scarlett walk into the lion's den. The man hadn't needed to tell him.

"I'm not just some damsel in distress that needs babysitting," Scarlett countered.

He should have seen that one coming.

"That's not what I'm saying," Officer Ramone said. "Not even close."

Emily walked over and put her hand on Scarlett's arm. "Sister, I know how tough you are. You're a Trapper. We just can't put you in any more danger than necessary. As it is, we are pushing the boundaries by having you up here on the trail with us."

"I told you there was no way I was staying behind," Scarlett said. She kept her tone low as though she didn't want to pick a fight but wanted to make it clear that she wasn't going to be kept in a corner. "And I do understand that my being here is a liability for your department, but like I told you before we left—Butch wants me. I'm your most powerful bargaining chip."

Emily nodded. "Which is why we need you safe. We are just going to go down to the cabin and see if there is even any credibility to the tip. If our vics are there, great. And if Butch is there and we need you, you will be the first to know. I promise. Just be patient with us. Okay?"

Miles took mental notes. Emily was good at talking down what could have been a potential problem. It made him feel better that she, Burns and Ramone were the ones going into that cabin. If there was any chance of a verbal resolution, Emily seemed like the best one to make that happen.

Scarlett sighed. "We will be here when and if you need us," she said, walking over to him and taking hold of his hand.

Emily sent him a toothy grin. "Thank you."

"Please, just come back with Kelcie and my brother."

Scarlett nodded. "I need to know she's okay."

Burns walked up beside Emily and whispered something into her ear. Her smile and the softness she'd had for them disappeared. "Guys we will do all we can. For now, the rest of our teams are about in place that are coming up from the other side. It's time. Promise me...don't go anywhere. Okay?"

They both nodded. "We will be here with the horses." Miles crossed his heart with his finger.

The officers huddled up and did a quick equipment check, and he could hear them going over some of their strategies about moving in on the cabin and clearing the building when they arrived, but he couldn't hear everything they were saying. Part of him wished that he could tag along and be a part of bringing down Butch. He would have given his figurative left foot for the chance after all the things that Scarlett had told him about the man.

As it was, though, this was an operation that, more than

anything, would rely on their getting lucky and getting to him at the right place and at the right time. In all reality Butch could have been anywhere, and they were just searching for a needle in a haystack.

The thought made him shudder.

If they could just get their hands on Jackson and Kelcie, that would be enough. At least, for now.

The cops disappeared into the timber, moving silently as they hiked toward the cabin and following the directions he had given them. Seagrass nickered as though she could sense the tension in the air.

He walked over to the horse, Scarlett's hand still in his, and ran his free hand down the horse's neck. "She's nervous," he said.

"The last time I was this anxious," Scarlett whispered, "I was working as an extra on this show about dogs for some educational programming station. It was a stupid job, really, something just to make some rent money and pad the portfolio."

"What did you do as an extra on a dog show?" he asked, chuckling lightly and more out of nerves than at the thought.

"I was supposed to walk the dogs out so they could be introduced by the professionals and discussed." She ran her hand down Seagrass's haunch. "It was such a silly thing, but it ended up being probably one of my most enjoyable roles to date. All I did was play with puppies all day long. And it empowered me in a way that made me want to stay in Hollywood for a really long time. And it's moments like those that led to this." She motioned around the woods.

Miles smiled. "I know you mean that like a bad thing, but not everything about this trip has been a complete bust. I mean…" He leaned in and gave her a kiss to her forehead. "I did get to meet you."

She caught his gaze. "That's the only thing about my life which is keeping me going right now—you. You have no idea how happy you make me."

His heart thrashed inside his chest. "And you made me realize that some people are worth fighting for—and trusting."

He moved a hair out of her face as he leaned in and kissed her lips. He took her into his arms. She tasted of sweat and dust, and he could imagine no headier mix—it epitomized his perfect love.

"I wish we had met under different circumstances. I hope you know, I would have asked you to stay with me, forever," he whispered into her hair. "But I know you have a life out there that doesn't involve me, and I'm crazy for thinking that last night meant anything."

"Don't talk like that," she said, pulling back and looking up into his eyes. "Last night meant something special to me, too. I don't just spend the night with anyone. I—"

"That's not what I meant," he said, not letting her continue.

She pulled loose from his arms and turned her back to him. "Just give me a minute, Miles." She motioned for him to stay put. "I won't go far. I just need to think." She pointed vaguely north.

He nodded, afraid to say anything out of the fear that if he did, she would tell him that he was right and that her life outside of their blink in time together was what mattered.

What he should have been thinking about was Jackson and Kelcie, but with them being put on the shelf, the only thing he could think about was Scarlett, and those thoughts were killing him.

Scarlett looked over her shoulder at him as she moved into the brush. He could have sworn there were tears on her cheeks, but he couldn't bear the possibility of him being right, and he looked away. The horses moved around him. Oreo sent him a white-eyed look and pawed at the ground with her front hoof nervously.

"I know, Oreo, I don't like it, either." He refused to look in Scarlett's direction.

He needed to get used to her leaving.

No. He couldn't do it. He couldn't stand idly by while she decided what she thought about him and what had gone on between them. He had to say his piece.

He charged off into the woods after her. His footfalls sounded loud and heavy as he hurried through the timber, weaving and bobbing as he followed her tracks. It only took a minute before he found her with her back turned to him, and the sight of her made his racing pulse calm.

"Scarlett?" he asked.

She turned and motioned for him to be quiet. Her face was an ashen white and her eyes were round with shock and fear. She wiggled her finger to come closer and to get low.

The momentary calm was replaced by a new sense of fear. He moved to her side. "What is it?" he whispered.

"Look," she said, pointing out to a creek bed where a beaver had built a dam and a small pond had formed.

Splashing around and laughing in the pond, bare-assed naked, was Kelcie, her arm tied up with his bandana, with a gray-haired and paunch-bellied man.

Jackson was nowhere to be seen.

SCARLETT DIDN'T KNOW what overtook her, but she finally knew what it meant to see red.

Kelcie moved into Butch's arms and threw her uninjured arm around his neck and planted a kiss on his pudgy fish lips. If she hadn't seen it with her own eyes, she would have never believed such a thing had really taken place. Kelcie had known everything that Butch had done, how he had harassed her and called her incessantly.

She had even been the one to help her navigate the chaos he had tried to create in her career with producers.

Now this?

She let out a tiny squeak of pain and panic as she thought about just how long Kelcie could have been with Butch and all the reasons why they would have ended up together.

She couldn't face it, she just couldn't.

Scarlett bent down and picked up a rock the size of her fist.

"What are you doing?" Miles asked.

"I'm going to kill him."

"No, Scarlett." Miles took her free hand and held on with all his might. "You can't become a criminal because of hate. I know the anger and rage you have to be feeling right now."

"My best friend… She went behind my back. She set this up. She had to have told him." The words came flooding out as she realized what must have happened. "We have to find Jackson."

She stared at him, but where the anger and rage had filled her there was a new sense of nothingness and merely the dissociation that came in moments of such complex emotions that the body took over.

It was in this moment that she truly understood how people who had never been driven to murder could kill.

"You just take out your phone. Remember, the police are watching it. Take a video. We will beat these jerks in court."

That wasn't enough, not for the sting of betrayal and anger she felt in her heart. Yet, her hands shook as she took out her phone and took the video of the two lovers playing and caressing each other. After a minute or so of recording, long enough to make bile rise in her throat, she sent off the video to Ramone, Burns and Emily and then sat her phone on the ground as it kept recording. It was strange, but it felt far heavier than the rock in her other hand. She couldn't watch any more.

Miles let go of her. He pulled the rock from her fingers. "Baby, you don't need this."

There was a strangled cry from the pond and the sound of splashing. "What in the hell are you two doing here?" Butch cried.

She turned to see Butch rushing to the edge and pulling a revolver from under his pile of clothes. He fumbled with the small silver gun.

Miles had a feral smile on his lips as he whispered to her, "Did I ever tell you that my favorite movie was *Braveheart*? Watch this." He pulled back his arm and hurled the rock.

It struck Butch right between the eyes as if the man had a bull's-eye painted on his face. The impact made a dull *thump* sound like that of a ripe watermelon. The pale bloated carp of a man dropped the gun in his hand and slipped down and under the water.

Kelcie looked at him, confused. "Butch? Baby? Are you okay?" She tried to pull at him and lift him from the water, but she struggled with his mass. "Butch. You can't die! Miles, what did you do?"

Though she wanted to watch Kelcie struggle and panic as Butch succumbed to the water in some poetic and cinematically perfect justice, her love for Miles surfaced.

"That was one hell of a throw." She smiled. "Remind me not to piss you off from a distance." She gave a slight laugh.

He smirked. "It's not the first time that skillset has come through for me, but usually it's helpful with hardheaded cattle and its squarely on the rump."

"Same difference." She tilted her head toward her enemies. "I don't want more problems." If Butch drowned, they had more than enough evidence that Miles had acted in self-defense, but she didn't want to make Miles have to be drawn into a lengthy possible homicide investigation for her.

As much as she hated the idea, she had to keep Butch and Kelcie alive. They had to face the judge for the things they had done.

"Stay behind me," Miles said.

Scarlett nodded. She didn't know if she would be able to control her mouth.

The moment Miles and Scarlett came out of the thicket of brush and into the open, Kelcie started to wail and scream. She rushed from the water, pointing back at Butch. "You have to help me! He...he took me!" she cried as she looked toward the gun as though she considered reaching for it and taking a shot.

Miles rushed to the gun and picked it up, dumping the rounds on the ground and stuffing the pistol into the back of his waistband.

Kelcie's clothes were on the ground beside the creek, and Scarlett grabbed her bloody shirt and threw it at her in disgust. "Cover yourself."

Miles moved past her, not even sparing her a wayward glance as he went to Butch and took his arm and yanked him from the water. He pulled him up onto the silty bank and dropped him haphazardly, facedown but able to breathe in the dirt.

Kelcie blubbered and sobbed as she tried to speak, but her words came out in unintelligible gibberish of the hysterical guilty. She put on the shirt, covering her nakedness, but only barely.

"Pull yourself together," Scarlett ordered. "Where's Jackson?"

Kelcie put her hand up in submission. Her hands were shaking. She dropped to her knees in the mud beside Butch.

"Jackson…" She hiccupped and pointed in the direction of the cabin where Emily and her team were investigating. "He's going to be okay. Butch said the drugs will wear off."

She sent Miles a look of guarded relief.

"When did you tell Butch we were here?"

Kelcie dropped her gaze to the ground. "As soon as we booked the trip."

"Why did you tell him? What was in it for you?" She looked at the pale, unconscious man. "Do you love him?" The thought made her nauseous.

Kelcie shook her head. "He told me he'd sell my screenplays. I saw what he did for your career." She started to cry again. "You know your career is coming to an end. What was I going to do?"

Scarlett balled her hands into tight fists as Miles stepped beside her and held her arms to her sides as though he could see how much she wanted to strike. "Not screw over your best friend."

Miles pulled her back. "Let's just restrain Butch and wait for the police. We have what we need. Don't make it worse."

She was so angry, she was the one shaking now. "I hate her. Do you know how much I did for her? We traveled around the world on my dime. She knew all my secrets." She paused. "Wait… Did you guys have something to do with Aiden and Thomas getting hurt?"

Kelcie didn't answer.

"Tell me!" Scarlett ordered.

"Butch thought the rental was yours." She shook her head. "They weren't supposed to be there."

"Kelcie, your selfishness cost a man his life, a boy his father, and now it will cost you your freedom. I won't even mention our friendship. I hope you both get what you deserve in prison."

Chapter Twenty-Five

"When you broke into the cabin on the West Glacier Cattle Ranch, were you hoping to find our witness, Ms. Leafletter?" the prosecuting attorney for the state asked Butch.

His puffy, pale face was covered in a layer of sweat, and a bead rolled down his temple and slipped to his chin. He dabbed it away with the back of his sausage-fingered hand. Everything about the man made Scarlett want to stand up and scream, but she was never again going to run away from the swine.

Kelcie was in an orange jumpsuit on the television screen, waiting but unable to hear or see what was happening in the courtroom until she was asked to take the stand.

"I didn't want to kill Scarlett. I just wanted to talk to her. She wouldn't take my calls."

"Objection!" his defense attorney countered.

Scarlett hated the courtroom games, and she barely listened as the defense attorney spoke to the judge. She couldn't understand why anyone would want to become a criminal defense attorney—or what kind of person would stand beside someone like Butch, a man who had knowingly and maliciously attacked with the intent to kill. It was unforgiveable.

Thankfully, before court had even started, and while the detectives had been questioning them about the stolen wallet and how Butch had broken into the cabin, it hadn't taken much for the two to turn on each other. Butch had pointed the finger at Kelcie for her complicity while Kelcie had told them about their plans—every detail, down to his desire for the ransom money to wipe out her savings and remind her of what he'd done for her financially, and then his wish to kill her in the end. Or, as Kelcie had put it, "If she refused to love him, then she didn't get to love anyone else—not after all he'd done for her."

Later, in front of the detectives, Kelcie had also admitted that they had planned on using the media frenzy created by Scarlett's death as a launching pad for her career. Everyone would want to talk to the dead actress's agent, and "*Bing, boom, bang*, she would be in," or so she had said.

Scarlett was no Julius Caesar, but she had her own Brutus.

According to the prosecutor, the trial was more of a formality, and at the end of the day, he would offer them both plea deals. If they took them, which they would most likely do, Butch would serve a minimum of fifteen years in a state prison without the chance for parole for his role in Aiden's death and her attempted murder.

Kelcie would serve a minimum of five years for her role as his accomplice.

When the judge called for a recess, she made her way from the courthouse, and Miles caught her outside. "How are you doing?" he asked.

He was wearing a dark suit, but it was such a juxtaposition from the man on the mountain she had met a few months ago that she had to stare for a long moment to make sense of exactly the man whom she was seeing. She couldn't help but smile. "I'm doing okay."

"Thomas called while you were on the stand. He says he can't wait for you to come home tonight," he said. "We're making elk spaghetti tonight. Jackson is sitting with him for now, until I get back."

After Aiden's death, Miles had taken over custody of Thomas, acting as his legal guardian. She'd been staying the occasional night with the duo while they had been awaiting trial.

"That sounds amazing," she said. Her phone vibrated in her pocket, and she took it out to take a peek at the message. It was an email from the agent she had reached out to in reference to the new season of *Rogue Crafter*. She wasn't sure if she was excited or reticent about opening the email that lay at her fingertips. Her future waited and could all change with this one tap.

The producer wanted to negotiate terms but was on the fence about bringing her back. It was a game, one only a good agent could help her navigate. If this agent didn't agree to work with her, her career would be over.

Part of her wanted to stay in Montana, to live in the world she had been holing up in, and where she had grown up. She had run away from the place because of her father, because of abuse and neglect, but she had faced her ghosts—the same ones that had followed her to every corner of the planet and back here. The one thing she had learned was that it didn't matter where she ran, or what role she played—the happiest she had been was at peace with Thomas and Miles.

This trial would pass, and she could go back to the life she had before, but she would be alone.

The thought made her feel incredibly lonely, and the pain was sharp.

"Everything okay?" Miles asked, pointing at the phone in her hands.

"It's the agent." She looked into his eyes. He knew how much was riding on this email—her future, their future,

Thomas's future. "I'm glad it came while we were standing together, but I'm not sure I'm ready to open it."

He smiled, but the action didn't quite reach his eyes. "No matter what you choose, I support your decision. I just want you to be happy."

"Miles, I'm happy with *you*." She leaned in and kissed him, the action gentle and sweet. "I love you."

He cupped her face in his warm hands and looked into her eyes. "And I love you, more than you will ever know. If you want to be together, I'll give up cowboying and I'll follow you around this planet."

"You can't do that to Thomas."

His expression faltered. "A boy can travel."

"Some is okay, but he also needs stability, and the ranch would provide that. My family would give him an incredible home. If I stayed."

"You want to stay?" he asked, sounding surprised.

"For you, and us, yes." She reached up and took his hand with her free hand.

"Would you want to be my wife?" he asked. It sounded like a question that had come out of the blue, nothing rehearsed, but something he had given great thought.

"In a heartbeat. Yes."

Though she had no idea what their future would bring, and she didn't care, their lips met and there was no on-screen kiss that could have compared, not even that of *Casablanca*.

He pressed his forehead against hers, half breathless. "Open the email."

She fumbled with her phone. "But what if—"

"It doesn't matter. We will figure it out," he said, cutting her off. "And I'm sorry I don't have a ring. I'll let you pick out anything you want as soon as we can."

She smiled as she opened up her phone. She didn't even

care about the ring. It was the furthest thing from her mind. Opening up the email, she read it aloud:

Dear Ms. Leafletter,
I'm excited to offer my representation for your upcoming series. I'm also excited to let you know I've been in talks with the producer, Mr. Anciaux, and he would be interested in filming on your family's ranch in Montana. Please give me a call to discuss. I have attached a contract. Please let me know if you have any questions.
Sincerely,
Adam Goldblum

She squealed with excitement as she dropped her phone and launched herself into Miles's arms.

For the first time in her life, she had it all, but most importantly, she had found the things she had been searching for the longest—security, family and love.

* * * * *